MW01225488

SHADOWS

A yacht cruise around Alaska and Canada was just what Dana needed to help her break out of her rut. Which was not, she knew, the only reason she was eager to join the party. It was also that from the moment she met Kurt Saunders she had the feeling that she could follow him to the ends of the earth ...

SHADOWS

BY
VANESSA GRANT

MILLS & BOON LIMITED
15 16 BROOK'S MEWS
LONDON W1A 1DR

First published in Great Britain 1986
by Mills & Boon Limited

© Vanessa Grant 1986

Australian copyright 1986

ISBN 0 263 11244 6

Set in Times 10½/10½pt
07-1186-49909

Computer typeset by SB Datagraphics,
Colchester, Essex

Printed and bound in Great Britain by
Collins, Glasgow

CHAPTER ONE

DANA HENDRICKS was on holiday. Incredible that a few short hours could take her across the water and half-way up Vancouver Island—far from rush hour traffic and the depressing solemnity of Mr Samuelson's office.

Mr Samuelson wouldn't have recognised his efficient, immaculately suited secretary as she boarded the *Tenaka* in faded denim jeans. Her hair was a golden cloud swirling about her face as she ran her old car up the ramp on to the inter-island ferry. Her skin was glowing, her grin too lively for the quiet law office where she spent her weekdays.

Two weeks away from the city was a gift of freedom. At dawn today, she had watched Vancouver disappearing on the horizon. Now she was almost home, waving to the sailor who was guiding the boarding cars.

'Home for a holiday, Dana? Go to the left, girl—park behind the red camper.'

'Thanks, Eric. Have a nice day.'

She parked and ran up, out on deck where she could see the ocean and feel the wind blowing the city air away. She had missed this so much! Not for the first time, she considered quitting her job, leaving the city to come home for good.

She smiled at a petite, elegant girl standing against the rail.

'Beautiful day, isn't it?' The woman's accent was faintly French, her frothy dress suitable for an afternoon cocktail party in the city.

'Beautiful,' Dana agreed.

5

'Hope it lasts. I've had it with rain! I'm Wendy Arunson.'

'Dana Hendricks. This is your first trip to the islands?'

'Yes. Wayne's doing the computer program for Kurt, so we're going on this sailing trip with Kurt and Andy.' Wendy was obviously in the habit of throwing strange names around like water. 'They have to test the thing, make sure it works. Wayne's my husband.'

'Real sailing? In a sailboat?'

'Yes. We're going up the islands. You know—the Queen Charlotte Islands—Alaska. Kurt's been sailing for years, ever since . . . He's been wildly successful with these inventions of his. It's Kurt's sailboat; he and Wayne put together this marvellous system. It's a— well, my mind goes blank when Wayne starts talking bits and bytes.'

'You're on your way to Sointula?' Her quiet village seemed an inappropriate setting for a crew of high-tech sailors.

Wendy set her curls in motion with a vigorous nod. 'I had to get the twins settled with Wayne's mom, so Kurt said they'd start out from Vancouver. Now they're waiting for me at Sointula. What about you, Dana? Going sailing?'

'Don't I wish! In two weeks I'll be back at work. I'm home for the holidays—visiting my parents on the lighthouse near Sointula.'

'A lighthouse? Did you grow up in the lighthouse? I grew up in the middle of Montreal. Were you lonely?'

She couldn't remember being lonely as a child, but she had been lonely often enough in the midst of the city.

'No. I've lived around here all my life. I lived in Sointula till I was sixteen, then on the lighthouse. While you're here, you must take a walk up behind the village;

it's fascinating up there. The old Finnish settlers built farmhouses, each with its own sauna. They usually built their saunas before the houses!'

'Well——' Wendy looked down at her flimsy sandals and Dana realised she wasn't about to go walking, exploring. 'The settlers—your ancestors? I could tell you were Finnish. You're so tall, and that gorgeous hair——'

There was no point contradicting her. 'The farmers are all fishermen now. Hardly any of the old farms are still producing.'

'Your father's not a fisherman?'

'Not any more.'

'And now you've left home? Where do you live? Married?'

'Not married. I work in a law office in Vancouver—— Nights I pound a typewriter, writing articles and trying to get them published.'

'You should write about our trip. Sailing, beautiful boat—romantic captain . . .'

'To really write about it, I should come along. I'd throw up my job in a minute for a trip like that!'

'You could ask Kurt, but I don't really think——'

'What does the boat look like? Tell me more about it.' It was only a dream, but she indulged herself, letting Wendy's chatter wash over her, listening as much to the images in her own head as to the words the other woman spoke.

'All vehicle owners return to the car deck,' droned the loudspeaker.

'You don't have a car, do you, Wendy? I'll give you a ride over to the government floats. Do you think I might get a look around?'

'Why not? I sure don't want to walk. These sandals are murder on my feet!'

'Will they be expecting you? Someone might come to

meet you at the ferry.'

'No. I wasn't sure which ferry I'd be catching.'

Wendy looked around as they drove off the ferry, then pronounced the village 'quaint'. It was only a minute's drive to the public floats. By that time Wendy had seen all she wanted of Sointula.

The ramp to the floats was steep, treacherous for anyone with dainty high heels. Wendy hung on to the rail, tottering as she eased her way down the ramp, cursing as her ankle turned in the fine straps of her sandals.

'How's the big city, Dana?' called up a fisherman from the float below.

'Fine, Jon. How's fishing?'

'Not very good this year. Getting a few, but that's all.'

'Last year, when you said the fishing was rotten, Christa got a new dishwasher!'

His young, weathered face creased in a grin. 'I've got to keep my favourite spots a secret. If I say there's no fish, nobody follows me!'

'Jon, this is Wendy Arunson, She's joining the people on the big sailboat.' Dana could see it already—too large, really, to be called a boat—perhaps too small to be a ship. She hadn't realised it would be so beautiful— the tall wooden masts staking a claim on freedom. She had never been on a sailboat in her life, but she loved this one at sight. Oh, she could write a story about that yacht if she had the chance! The glistening white hull with the rich teak rails. Teak decks, too, she decided, although she couldn't tell that yet—not until she was closer.

'Those masts are—they must be over fifty feet tall! And surely that's not—who's up there? At the top of the mast?'

'That's Kurt!' Wendy tipped her head back and

yelled, 'Hey, Kurt! Hi!'

'I hope no one shouts at me like that when I'm up a tall pole,' muttered Jon, wincing and looking up uneasily.

'He's waving back to her. If it was me, I'd be hanging on with both hands. Mind you, he seems to be keeping his attention on the job.'

'Come off it, Dana! You're the girl who climbed up on to the school roof back in grade two—I remember old Herbert going up there to get you down. He was frightened out of his mind, but you weren't. You were laughing!'

'What's he doing up there?' she asked, not really expecting that Jon would have the answer, but not surprised when he did.

'Radio problems. He's working on his antenna.'

'How did he get up?'

'Andy—his crew—and I hauled him up with a halyard winch about an hour ago. As far as I could make out, the captain finds climbing up there pretty routine.'

Dana wasn't surprised that Jon had made friends with the captain of the sailboat and was offering him a helping hand. Most of the fishermen were ready and willing to offer help to another seaman.

'He had a look at my autopilot yesterday,' Jon told her. 'I don't know what he did, but it's working for the first time in years.'

'Are you sure it's all right for you to leave now? What if he wants to come down?'

'They tell me that getting down is the easy part.'

Wendy was walking ahead, eager to get aboard.

'Tell Christa I'll stop by next week.' The man at the top of the mast was coming into focus as she came closer, his muscular, golden-tanned back rippling as he worked high above her.

'How are you getting home?' Jon asked from behind her.

'I was going to find a radio and call Dad to come for me. Can I use your radio?'

'Don't do that. I've got a load of supplies to bring down from my car, then I'll take you in the herring skiff.'

'Thanks, Jon. I'll see you in a few minutes, then.'

Wendy was ahead of Dana, stumbling as she jumped on to the deck, causing the man above her to swing out from the mast on his rope.

'Hey! Who's rocking the boat? Cut it out!' His voice was deep and resonant and, at the moment, sounded understandably jumpy.

Wendy disappeared inside the vessel quickly, without answering.

'It was Wendy getting on the boat. She's just gone inside.' Dana had to walk back to look up and see his face.

He was rugged-handsome, his fair hair sun-bleached over a darkly tanned face that gave an impression of hard lines.

'You're a friend of Wendy's?'

'I gave her a ride from the ferry. Are you sure you won't fall, leaning over like that?'

'Don't worry. I'm well tied into this chair. If you're going to get on to this ship, step carefully, would you? A little rocking down there is a pretty big swing up here. Would you know how Wendy's trip went?'

'She didn't mention any problems. I'll stay on the wharf. Are you doing anything special up there? Or is it just the view that attracts you?'

The view is pretty spectacular, but I've seen about enough of it for now. Keep clear while I lower these tools.'

He lowered a plastic bucket tied to the end of a rope.

When it had settled on the deck, he asked, 'Could you untie that and move it out of the way?'

Dana stepped carefully on to the deck, trying not to cause any unnecessary motion.

'Just the line on the bucket. Don't touch any others.'

'I won't.' She looked up at the soles of his deck shoes and the bottom of the bo'sun's chair. 'You're tied to the rope that's on this big cleat on the mast? I won't touch it.'

'Do I sound nervous? I'm in rather a vulnerable position. I can't see what you're doing down there.'

She turned at the sound of a footfall on the deck, found herself staring at a bushy red beard below laughing dark eyes and an unruly thatch of dark hair.

'Hi. You're Dana? I'm Andy. Wendy said you were here, but she didn't tell me——'

'Is that you, Andy? called the captain from above.

'It's me. In person. Are you ready to come down and join us common folk?'

'The sooner the better. My leg's gone to sleep.'

Dana stepped quickly out of the way as Andy moved to the mast and started loosening the line on the cleat.

'Too fast?' Andy asked as he let the line slide on the winch drum. He looked like a reckless youth, but he was handling the line with care.

'Faster if you like,' came back the voice from above.

He came down only inches away from her. When his feet hit the deck, he stood up, almost touching her, with rope and the bo'sun's chair hanging around him and deep blue eyes burning down at her. Staring up at him, she felt strangely breathless.

He was taller than she had thought, long and lean and obviously accustomed to the sun. For a moment, they were so close that she could feel the heat coming off him, then he stepped back and she was on the outside, watching the two men efficiently clearing up lines and tools.

'You fixed it?' asked Andy.

The fair head nodded. 'The fitting was badly corroded. No wonder we had problems.' He rubbed the back of his leg where the wooden edge of the chair had cut a deep red mark on his skin.

'There's coffee.'

'Good!' He turned to Dana, bringing her close with a warm smile. 'You'll join us?'

'Thanks. I'd love a chance to see inside.'

'If you say nice things about this ship, you can come for coffee any time you like.' Dana found her lips curving as her eyes met the quiet humour in the depths of his.

'I'm Dana Hendricks,' she told him, watching the laughter lines at the sides of his mouth. He had a strong face that knew how to laugh. Yet, when the smile faded, he looked strangely remote and sombre. She found herself casting about mentally for something to say, to make him smile again.

Inside, she found herself seated across from Wendy at a glowing mahogany table, watching as Andy poured steaming mugs of coffee for them all.

'I'm Wayne,' said the dark man who had his arm around Wendy. 'Thanks for giving my wife a ride.' His voice was intense, as if thanks were something he had trouble expressing.

'This is my reward—getting inside. I was hoping to see this boat.'

'This is not a boat,' Andy corrected with a flash of white teeth through the beard. 'Any ship that is big enough to carry a tender can't be called a boat. The dinghy's a boat—this is a yacht.'

'Forgive my slip.'

Kurt asked, 'Have you ever been sailing?'

'Never. What's it like?'

'That depends who you ask.'

'If I ask you?'

'I'm biased. I'd tell you it's marvellous . . . fresh wind in the sails as you steal out of an isolated bay in the early morning. The sea moving under your feet, carrying you on a journey of discovery. The only trouble is,' and he grinned at her with sudden laughter, 'that it's addictive. You get hooked, can't keep away from the water.'

'I have a cousin who's hooked on climbing glaciers.' Dana looked around at their faces. 'This seems like more fun. Warmer, too.'

Wendy sat up suddenly in the circle of Wayne's arm. 'He's not telling you the bad parts. When it rains for three days and everything gets wet. The wind's blowing and you're cold and seasick.'

'I told you I was biased. Fortunately, I don't get seasick. Wendy does, and that can be miserable. But when you're really cold and wet, you pull into some isolated little harbour where there's a natural hot spring and have a hot bath on nature.'

'Are you selling tickets? If so, you've got a buyer. I've never been on a sailboat before. I'm used to fishing boats. Fishermen call *their* boats *boats*. But this one—yacht, ship—isn't quite what I expected. I understood the inside was filled with high-tech equipment.'

Wayne laughed. 'I see you've heard about Kurt and his love of gadgets.'

'Computerised everything. That's what I heard.'

Kurt was putting cream and sugar on the table, then he slipped into the seat beside Dana. 'It's all here,' he told her. 'Computers. All the bells and whistles—but I've tried to keep it concealed. Sailboats are supposed to be traditional.'

'You've succeeded—the teak and mahogany, polished oak floors. Well, perhaps the microwave oven in the galley isn't exactly traditional.'

'Or the video and television in the salon?' Kurt volunteered. 'It's true that I have a weakness for electronic gadgets.'

'I did see a radar antenna outside.'

'If you noticed that, you must be a sea-going girl,' he smiled.

'More of a sea*side* girl. My dad used to fish, but I didn't get to go with him very often. I've lived around here all my life, though. This is a fishing village; most of our friends are fishermen.'

Dana looked around at all of them. They seemed a strange assortment. Andy looked as if he would be most at home dressed in a leather jacket, riding a Harley Davidson. Wayne had the fine-drawn features of a perpetual student or an engineer. Wendy belonged in an ornately impractical modern home, welcoming important guests for dinner while the mother's help kept the children out of trouble upstairs.

Kurt defied such easy analysis. He had the tanned fitness and the strong face of a sailor. He also had an easy, confident charm that struck her as metropolitan. She was watching him, probing without realising it. His eyes met hers and for an instant she saw into their depths before the blue turned icy cold.

'Tell me about your trip, Kurt,' she said quickly. 'Where are you going? And why? It's not just a holiday, is it?'

'It's partly a holiday. We're going up the coast to Alaska, then across to the Queen Charlotte Islands. It's beautiful country. I've wanted to make this trip for a long time. It's partly business, too. The West Coast has some of the most challenging waters in the world; it's an ideal area to test out the computerised navigation system Wayne and I have been working on.'

'Don't let him fool you,' Wayne told her. 'Kurt

designed it. He did the engineering and wrote the pseudocode. All I did was——'

'An incredibly tricky job of programming that two other programmers had already told me was impossible.'

'You wouldn't have space on board for one more crew member, would you? I could pull lines or whatever it is sailors do—scrub the decks, polish the brass. And I'm a writer. I could write articles about your trip and this system of yours—get you publicity.' She was at least half serious.

'I'll keep it in mind if I come up short of crew,' he promised lightly, getting to his feet. 'Coffee break's over, Andy. I need a hand with the water.'

'Could I see the computer first? Before you go back to work.'

'I don't——' he began, then shrugged and changed it to, 'why not? It's back here.'

He led her back through a narrow corridor to the aft cabin.

'So this is where you hide the high-tech stuff.'

'This is it.' She recognised some of it. The radar, the marine radio, an autopilot control. 'We've fed that into the computer,' he explained, describing the system in layman's terms that she found easy to follow.

'A friend of mine has this kind of computer.'

'You can buy them in almost any department store. We've linked everything together. The secret is really in the software. Wayne doesn't like to blow his own horn, but he's made an incredible job of this. Here, sit down and I'll show you how easy it is to use.'

Kurt turned on the unit, his arm brushing hers as he reached across to adjust a knob. That casual contact sent electricity along her skin. She shivered, then met his eyes with a shock. They had turned a cool, icy blue again.

He showed her how to program a course into the computer. 'Good, that's it. If I pull out from the wharf and punch that up, we'll go to Port Hardy. I won't have to touch the wheel again until we dock.'

'You're leaving Monday?'

'That's right. At first light. Will you wave to us from the lighthouse?'

'If I can't talk you into letting me come. It's true that I'm a writer, and I'd love to come along and write about your cruise, your computer system.' He was starting to say no, so she went on quickly, 'Tomorrow, if you've time, why don't you all come over to the lighthouse. You could have a tour of the station, and my father would love to talk autopilots with you. And Mother makes wonderful fresh-baked cinnamon rolls.'

'Your mother wouldn't know what she was getting into—Andy can eat anyone's kitchen bare in minutes!'

'Mom likes big appetites,' she said truthfully. 'So do try to come.'

'We'll see.' He wasn't promising and she had to leave it at that. It was obviously time she left and let him get back to work.

The roar of Jon's outboard motor drowned out the few words they spoke to each other as they sped out of the bay and towards Pulteney Point. As they neared the point, Jon headed in to shore where the lighthouse and the red and white buildings marked the shallows for mariners.

'You'll come up for coffee? Mom would love to see you.'

'Next time,' he promised. 'I'll bring Christa next week.'

Dana found her mother in the garden, bent over the weeding, two dramatic wings of white streaking through her dark hair, the outline of the white lighthouse buildings behind her.

Sherrie Hendricks looked up—she had been looking up at Dana ever since her daughter turned eleven. 'Darling! You're early! I didn't expect you until tonight. How lovely! No, don't hug me, not yet, I'm all over with garden dirt. How was the trip?'

'Nice. I got up early. A lovely drive up Vancouver Island—goreous day! Where's Dad?'

'In the engine room. Go and tell him you're home. Are you hungry? Did you have lunch?'

'Just some apples I brought with me. I could eat a horse.'

'Some day, Dana, that appetite will catch up with you. Now, go off and find your father. I'll dig out some smoked salmon.'

He was in the engine room, bent over something at the workbench. She watched him for a moment, seeing his tall lean body with its heavily-muscled torso only partly concealed by the loose shirt he wore. His once-blond hair was mostly grey now, had been for years. When he moved, she saw the limp that had been with him for eight years, ever since the stormy night when he had slipped on the log, falling into the wild water between the log and the boat.

The noise from the generators masked Dana's approach, but he wasn't startled when he turned and saw her. He smiled and put out a hand to touch her.

She shouted against the noise, 'Mom says to bring you in for coffee!' He nodded, not wasting his lungs trying to talk over the generators.

She watched him as he put away his tools, then they left the building—he limping, she slowing her usual swift stride to match his.

Outside, she took his arm.

'You're looking good,' he told her.

'So are you. You have no idea how nice it is to be with someone tall! All day I've been with small people. I ran into a girl on the *Tenaka*—she was tiny! Then Mother—I feel like a giant!' But Kurt was tall, at least as tall as her father.

'Tall people get a better view of the world.'

'Of course we do,' she agreed. 'This girl on the ferry was going sailing. There's a big ketch in Sointula harbour—*Windflower II*. She was joining her husband—he's working for the owner—heading for parts unknown. I got on board for a look; she's a beautiful boat!'

'I remember an article about a *Windflower* in one of the sailing magazines a few years back. Fellow invented a new type of propeller.' Bruce Hendricks had a photographic memory that could be depended upon to dig out facts everyone else had long since forgotten.

'Is that so? Nobody mentioned propellers, but the owner's working on a computerised autopilot. And Wendy—the girl I met—said something about inventions.'

They climbed the stairs together. He opened the door for her and she preceded him into the kitchen.

'Must be the same fellow. *Windflower*, it was, but a smaller boat. That must have been ten years ago. His name was Saunders. An interesting fellow.'

'Kurt Saunders. I invited them over for a look at the lighthouse tomorrow—I don't know if they'll come.'

Dana's mother had laid out a feast on the kitchen table—salmon, cheese, fresh-baked bread. Dana started building a hearty sandwich.

'Kurt?' her mother speculated. 'A friend of yours, Dana?'

'No, Mother; I've barely met the man. He's the owner of a big sailboat in at Sointula. I offered to go with them—write articles about the trip and this autopilot for publicity.'

'Surely you wouldn't do that, Dana? How long is this

trip? You'd lose your job——'

'Don't worry, Mother. It was just wishful thinking on my part. Mind you, if I was asked I'd go quickly enough.' Her father was watching her thoughtfully, as if he knew what she was planning. Her mother was frowning.

'What about Harold—the nice boy you brought home at Christmas? Surely he wouldn't approve of your going away like that!'

Harold, at thirty, would choke to hear himself described as a boy.

'He's left Vancouver—managing a hotel in Queen Charlotte City.'

'Oh, but surely you're writing to each other?'

'Not yet. Maybe a christmas card. We're friends, Mother. It's not a big romance. It never will be,'

'It's no laughing matter, Dana. You're twenty-five now. Sooner or later you have to——'

'Later,' she suggested, smiling at her father. He was in no hurry to see her married.

After her father gave the late weather report on the radio, he joined her mother in their bedroom and Dana slipped down into the small room in the basement where her old typewriter still occupied a place of honour on the big desk.

She worked until long past midnight, then she slipped quietly up to bed.

She dreamed that she took passage on a sailing ship with a tall blond captain. In her dream, Kurt Saunders' eyes caught fire whenever they looked at her, but morning came and she found herself in her own bed, still on the lighthouse.

'So much for dreams.'

Once she had breakfast, she went out to help her father with the painting.

The visitors came when she was half-way up the

light-tower in a bo'sun's chair, a paint sprayer in her hands, long legs and bare feet dangling down from the chair, the noise of the compressor in her ears.

Then the compressor stopped, her sprayer stopped sending a fine jet of paint, and she looked down into Kurt Saunders' blue eyes. His slight smile told her he hadn't missed a detail of her tousled appearance.

'Your turn for the high places, is it?'

She shifted the sprayer in her hands so she could see him more easily. 'After watching you yesterday, I couldn't wait to try it myself.'

'Hi, Dana!' Wendy came up behind Kurt, her hand linked with her husband's. Behind Wendy, Andy's red beard grinned up at her. 'My God! I didn't expect to see you up there! Aren't you terrified?'

'It beats typing letters in a lawyer's office.' She used her feet to stand off from the tower as her father let her down. At the bottom, she scrambled out of the bos'un's chair in paint-splattered disarray, reaching out a hand to keep from falling into Kurt. His hands steadied her, sending goose-bumps along her bare shoulders.

'You're really getting into the holiday spirit, aren't you? Some people laze about on their holidays.' He looked up at the smooth white surface of the tower.

'It's a yearly ritual—if it doesn't move, we paint it.'

'How are you with varnish? I've got a lot of varnish work to be done.'

'I could learn.'

Her father took the sprayer out of her hands. 'I'm going to take the men around the station. Tell your mother we'll be up for coffee in a few minutes.

'If I know Mother, she's already got the buns in the oven. Would you like to come, Wendy?' Wendy would be happier chatting with Mrs Hendricks over a cup of coffee than looking at generators and foghorns.

Dana headed for the shower, emerging moments

later looking cool in blue shorts and a cotton top, her hair tied back loosely. In the kitchen, she found that Wayne and Andy had arrived. Andy was staring at the oven door, his nose twitching above the beard.

'Kurt warned me about you. He said you'd eat everything on the table.'

'Can you believe that brother of mine—blackening my name, spreading rumours! It's all lies—but while Kurt and your father are involved in deep, technical consultation on the lawn, I plan to beat him to the cinnamon rolls!'

She would never have guessed that Kurt and Andy were brothers. Kurt's smooth blond hair surely came from a different gene pool than the dark riot on top of Andy's head.

'There's plenty for all of you.' Sherrie Hendricks was pleased by the good-humoured wrangling over her baking. She loved company, loved feeding people. 'Dana, take coffee out to your father and Mr Saunders. Does anyone know what he takes in his coffee?'

'Sugar and cream.'

'Thanks, Andy. Dana, tell them the buns will be out of the oven in five minutes.'

First Dana stopped to pick up her scrapbook.

She found them at the picnic table, bent over a piece of paper. Her father was tracing along one line with a finger.

'It's an idea,' Kurt agreed. He smiled for Dana, shifting to make room for her beside him. 'It would be easy enough to make the modification, especially at this stage.'

'Coffee here,' announced Dana. 'and cinnamon rolls in five minutes. Has Dad redesigned your system yet, Kurt?'

'Some good ideas,' His darkly tanned hand followed the line her father had traced. 'I'll think about that,

Bruce. It might just be the thing to do.' He smiled again at Dana, 'I'm glad you invited me.'

'So am I. Are you all set for your trip now?'

'Almost. We'll be leaving tomorrow morning.'

'How long will you be gone?'

His eyes took on a faraway look. 'We'll be back in Vancouver in early October.'

'Four months. Have you reconsidered taking a journalist on board? I'd love to write up your trip.'

'Lots of people sail up the West Coast. It's not news.'

Her father was watching, quietly amused. He had known last night that she was up to something.

'But your trip is different enough to catch the interest of readers. And if you don't take advantage of its publicity value, you'll miss a lot of sales later when the system goes on the market.'

'Sailing articles are pretty technical—so's this navigation system.'

'If you and Wayne explain it to me, I can write it. Kurt, look at these.' She opened the scrapbook in front of him. 'Articles I've written. See if——'

'You talk as if there's a job you're applying for. There isn't a job.'

'If I can talk you into it, there will be—look, forget that for a minute. Just read the articles—see what you think!'

Her mother had faithfully pasted every one of her published articles into the scrapbook. Dana found herself holding her breath as Kurt turned the pages.

Sun-bleached hair had fallen across his forehead. His shirt was open at the neck. She could see a sparse sprinkling of fair hair glistening against the tan. What would it feel like to touch him there, to run her fingers over the contours of his chest?

When he turned to the article she had written for the yachting magazine, he started to laugh, the rich sound of his deep voice a great relief to her.

'Is this true?' He gestured to the page he was reading. 'Nicotine fit', the article was entitled.

'Oh, yes, it's true. Ask Dad.'

He shook his head in amazement. 'I can just picture the captain of that ferry when he was flagged down by this crazy lighthouse-keeper. He must have thought he was rescuing the victim of a shipwreck. Imagine his feelings when he was asked for a package of cigarettes from the ship's canteen!'

'You don't smoke?'

'I used to. Crazy habit, but I had a time quitting it.' He reached down to turn another page, looking at an article she had done for a radio magazine, and his brows lifted, because it was a technical magazine.

Dana reached across to turn the pages to where she had slipped last night's work into the book. Her father was watching her. He said nothing, but she saw faint traces of worry in his blue eyes.

Kurt was silent a long moment after he put the pages down.

'Do you think the yachting magazines would go for it?'

'I could find out. In the morning I could go into Sointula and make some phone calls.'

Kurt frowned, studying Dana's face as if it could tell him something he'd missed until now. 'If I took you along, let you write these articles, what sort of arrangement would you expect?'

'Just my passage, and the rights to whatever I write.'

'I'd want final approval of your copy. The technical details have to be right.' His blue eyes were bottomless, seemed to stare right through her.

'Of course.'

Her father said, 'Dana has a good mind for technical details. She and I took our radio amateur tickets together. You don't pass those ham exams without good knowledge of electronics.'

'So that explains the radio article,' mused Kurt. He considered her silently for a moment, then smiled ruefully. 'You're a hard girl to say no to, Dana Hendricks. I've got to admit you make it sound pretty reasonable. But—what about your job? Your lawyer expects you back at work in Vancouver soon, doesn't he?'

'I've got two weeks' holiday right now. I'll phone him in the morning, give two weeks' notice.' Her father wasn't saying anything. She knew he wouldn't try to stop her, but her mother was going to raise the roof when she heard.

Her mother would say that jobs weren't easy to come by these days. She could see the same comment in Kurt's eyes.

'Journalism is what I want to do—it's what I've always wanted. And this trip you're making—if I missed it, I'd regret it all my life.' Their eyes met for a long, breathless moment, then he nodded abruptly.

'If you get any interest from the magazines, then all right—you can come. If you're going into Sointula for the phone tomorrow morning, you might as well come on board after your calls. We'll leave at noon and anchor off the point here—either to drop you off home, or for you to pick up your gear.'

CHAPTER TWO

SHE left early the next morning, stopping only to reassure her mother that she hadn't completely lost her sanity. Her father launched the speedboat for her, then Dana donned a lifejacket, started the engine, and went pounding across the bay towards Sointula in the choppy seas—a rough ride, but fast.

She passed the government wharf and pulled into a private landing farther up the beach. Christa, with her baby for an alarm clock, was always awake early.

'Of course you can use our phone, Dana, but not until you've had a cup of coffee!' Christa pushed Dana into a chair and poured a cup of coffee from the pot that was always sitting on her stove. 'Jon said he saw you. Now tell me the news! It's been so long!'

You couldn't rush Christa. She had to have her gossip. and she had some good ideas for Dana. 'Call the fishermen's magazines, too. Here, Jon always reads this one, and somewhere there's—yes, here it is. This one——'

The calls paid off. One of the fishing magazines could not have cared less about Kurt's system, but the other was definitely interested in a technical article on the system and its possible commercial applications.

Dana also found a yatching magazine which was willing to look at a series on the cruise, and Warren, the programme director for the Vancouver radio station, to whom she sometimes sold work, was interested in a series of commentaries on the seaside communities she would visit along the way—if she made the trip.

'Well, he can hardly turn you down now,' pronounced Christa as Dana hung up the phone at last. Christa hadn't even pretended not to listen. 'You'll make his system famous!'

Might he have changed his mind overnight? She worried about that as she pulled the speedboat up in the empty berth behind *Windflower II* and found Kurt scrubbing his decks—until she saw him smile when he saw her.

'She's already beautiful,' she greeted him. 'You don't need to pretty her up.'

'She won't be beautiful for long if I neglect her. You're looking pleased with yourself this morning. Am I right in supposing that I have a new crew member? Yes, well, come aboard. We may as well tow your speedboat back to the lighthouse and you can pick up your gear.'

Dana stayed on deck as they sailed across to Port Hardy, rocking as the yacht lifted gently on the waves, the sails out far to the sides to catch the light wind. Wing 'n' wing, Kurt had called it, letting out the mainsail to port and the mizzen to starboard, just like two wings of a white bird.

She had her notebook out, the pages going wild in the wind as she made notes for the first article, still having trouble believing that she had managed to get aboard for the trip.

'Give me a hand with this sail, Andy!' Kurt called as she watched him come out on deck, balancing against the easy motion as he walked. She watched the two men changing the forward sail for a larger one, making sure she didn't get in their way.

Down below was the small single cabin Kurt had shown her only an hour ago. Her pack was stored under the bunk, her clothes in hatches above the foot of the bunk.

'Andy was using this cabin,' he had told her, 'but I moved him last night. I thought you would need this desk. Later, I'll install the small computer here for you to use as a word processor.'

'And Andy?'

'He has a berth in the navigation room, It's comfortable, so don't worry about him. Wendy and Wayne are in the cabin just ahead of you, and my cabin is the one just behind the galley. Stow your gear, then ask Wendy to show you how the head and the shower work. We have running hot and cold water, but go easy on it.' He was backing out of the cabin as he talked, gone before she could ask why Andy had moved last night, before Kurt knew the results of her queries.

Wendy gave her a tour of the plumbing, heating and cooking features of life aboard this ship. Dana learned how to flush the toilet, how to use the shower, and how to light the kerosene stove.

'Not at all like cooking at home,' Wendy told her. 'The oven is terrible—hot on the top and not so hot on the bottom. I use the microwave mostly. We all take turns cooking—and doing dishes! I'll make up a new schedule now that you're here.'

'Kurt takes a turn, too?'

'Everybody! No kidding, Kurt insists. If the Queen came aboard. Kurt would have her take her turn at the dishes. We all have another jobs, too. Kurt and Andy look after the boat; Wayne programs the system when Kurt wants changes; I keep house, but we're all supposed to clean up our bunks as soon as we get up— and no mess lying around! Kurt says there's lots of room on a boat if you don't leave mess!'

'Sounds reasonable,' Dana agreed.

'Sailing's great—except when it gets rough. If you're smart you'll do what I do. When the storms start, I take a Valium and crawl into my bunk until it's over. Let the men do the worrying.'

'What if it's your turn to cook?' Wendy was young
and healthy. From what Dana could see, life had been
good to her. Surely she didn't need tranquillizers to help
her through a bad day?

'Who cares? Nobody feels like eating when we're
bouncing around—when we get to Port Hardy I'm
supposed to do the shopping while Kurt fuels up. I've
got a list as long as your arm. You'll come and help,
won't you?'

Helping Wendy meant pushing the cart, selecting the
groceries and listening to the perpetual chatter. The
grocery list was made out in firm, angular handwriting:
Kurt's writing, she decided. They filled the cart to the
brim and took a taxi back to the wharf.

Dana was amazed at the amount of food that could
be concealed on board. Tins went into hatches under
the seats, under the floor—in any corner that wasn't
used for some other purpose.

When everything was stowed, the boat fuelled and
the engine oil changed, they set off, waving goodbye to
the men on the deck of a red and white Coast Guard
cutter as they steamed past and left Hardy Bay.

'Port Alexander,' Kurt told her, 'That's as far as
we're going tonight. That'll give us a good start
tomorrow for crossing Queen Charlotte Sound.'

'We're going up the inside passage?'

'I'd like to go outside, up Hecate Strait, but we don't
have the right crew. Wendy and Wayne have only been
out for the odd weekend—and you've never sailed
before.'

'I'll have to learn to sail. I could take watches too.'

Dana would readily have taken back those words the
next day. By the time they came into Queen Charlotte
Sound, the sails were tight in the wind, pushing the
boat far over to starboard. The winds howled in the

rigging, promising a rough ride.

They had started by sailing easily in light winds. Then, as they came into the open, the wind had built and built and the waves gone wild. Dana's world turned upside down with the violent action of surging up one side of each wave, then falling down the other.

She found herself standing alone in the galley, holding on for dear life as the boat careened wildly and the floor tilted away from her. She was gripping a handrail built into the ceiling. Earlier, she had wondered why anyone would put rails on the ceiling!

Her legs were stiff, arms tense, eyes staring at the porthole on the other side of the boat where the water surged up over the glass.

She couldn't remember ever being so terrified, except once when she was small. A cousin had taken her on the big ferris wheel. When the wheel was stopped, with Dana at a dizzying height at the top, he had started to rock their seat.

'If you rock these seats far enough,' he told her with an evil grin, 'they come right out of their sockets.'

She had cowered, frozen, in her corner, waiting for the fall that would send her crashing to the ground. Later, on the ground, she had realised he had conned her. She'd run back into the queue and gone back up on the wheel.

When Kurt found her, she was huddled in the uphill corner of the galley in an echo of that remembered terror. He approached slowly, slipping his hand into the handrail just next to hers. He stood easily, one hip rested against the edge of the counter, forming a barrier between her and the floor that tilted away so alarmingly. His eyes watched her intently.

'Scared?'

She nodded, unwilling to make even that small motion, her body tensed hard against the forces of gravity that would send her crashing downhill. The yacht pitched, rocking, sliding down the side of a wave, then tilting back up with a crazy lurch as they hit the water at the bottom of the wave.

'Of course I'm scared!' She felt foolish, looking at his slight smile. He wasn't frightened, not even nervous! 'We're going to go over any minute! We'll probably sink!'

He shook his head, riding the turbulence easily. 'We won't, you know. But you have to learn to relax, ride with it.'

'Where's Wendy?' she whispered.

'In her bunk. Wendy has her own way of dealing with things.' He smiled at her. 'From what I've seen of you, I don't think it's your way. Do you want to go to your bunk?'

She felt a sudden longing for any kind of escape. Could she lie in her bunk, eyes closed, denying the reality of the sea?

It might have been possible, if it hadn't been for Kurt's eyes challenging her, making escape impossible.

'I'm not going to pretend this isn't happening.'

'Good girl! Come on up top.' His free hand was on her arm, urging her towards the stairs.

The world was tilted to an angle God had never meant her to feel. If she went outside, she would be completely exposed, looking right down into the water as they careened on the surface of the ocean.

She pulled back, panicking.

'If I go out there, I may be swept overboard. Look at the way we're titled. Any minute, we'll go right over!'

'Believe me, this ship is doing what she was built to do—sailing, using the wind. Come up and see.'

Dana shook her head stubbornly.

Kurt put his hands on her shoulders and gave her a slight shake. 'Do you want me to go away and let you be terrified in peace?'

'I—yes, I suppose that is how I feel. Terribly cowardly, aren't I? All right, I——' Her laugh was cut abruptly short as they tilted crazily. Her feet slid away from her. She grabbed hard on to the rail and the counter, sliding right into Kurt, and felt a warm shock as his arm went around her midriff.

'Who's steering this thing?' she asked.

'The autopilot, actually, but Andy's on watch. Now, come and learn something about sailing.'

She was too busy being terrified to fight him any longer. She followed, holding the walls and the rails, stumbling up the stairs behind him, into the cockpit where she was thrown against the side.

She landed in an unoccupied corner and stayed there. Once more she was on the uphill side, fighting gravity. She braced her legs and gripped the edge of the cockpit, hanging on so tightly that her arm began to tremble.

Andy shouted over the noise of wind and water, 'Isn't this great? Great sailing!'

'I'll take over,' Kurt told him. 'Go down and see about some coffee. I haven't had a cup in hours.'

'It's my watch, Kurt. Wendy's supposed to——'

'It's far too rough for Wendy to be cooking. Coffee, Andy—please.'

Andy shrugged and disappeared below, sliding the hatch closed with a bit of a bang, leaving Dana and Kurt alone on the wild sea.

Kurt caught Dana's troubled glance. 'Andy still has twinges of adolescent rebellion now and then, but they don't last. He'll be smiling again next time you see him.'

As they slid down the side of each wave, the deck was tilted almost vertically. Holding herself into the uphill corner by willpower and shaking muscles, Dana watched the sea come crashing towards them time and time again.

'Come here,' Kurt ordered gently as a big wave pounded on the hull. Perhaps she didn't hear at all, but his lips formed the words. As they rode up on to the top of a wave, he reached across and drew her over to him.

'It isn't nearly as bad as you think.' He spoke softly in her ear. She was cradled against his chest, his arm around her waist. They were on the low side now, with Kurt leaning into the corner of the cockpit. He kept her securely in the curve of his arm so that her body only pressed harder against his when they surged down the side of each wave.

'The first thing you have to do is stop fighting. Fear and tension go together. And the fear is really only in your mind.' His arm had slipped up to rub her trembling muscles gently. 'Relax—there's no percentage in fighting it.'

It was easier, leaning against him, feeling some kind of security in his arms. But her world was still tilted, unnatural.

'Thank you for not telling Andy that I was afraid.'

'You won't be afraid once you get used to it.'

'Couldn't the boat go right over? If the wind gets any worse——'

'This ship can take it. It's the people who sometimes have a problem. Now, relax, and look at the sails. She was built for this. Just watch.'

Dana looked up to where the sails billowed out hard to the starboard side, each one seeming to overlap the other, the wind funnelling through them.

'Have you ever been out in rough water on your dad's fishing boat?'

'Once. But with the stabilisers out, it wasn't like this. We were pounding into it, but not tipped over like this.'

'The fishing boats use stabilisers because they can't afford to tip over like this. They're not built to work with the wind, not like a sailboat. Sailboats are designed to take advantage of wind, to be at their best when it blows.'

While she was pressed against his chest, each wave pushed her softness against his muscular torso. When he reached for the autopilot override button and altered their course slightly, she felt the muscles ripple against her shoulder, felt the vibration from his low voice. She realised that her heartbeat had slowed its fearful thundering, her breathing had steadied.

'Watch the sails now. There's a gust coming, and the sails will fill harder. We'll heel a bit more, then we'll surge ahead.'

Dana shivered. The thought of heeling more was not reassuring.

'Remember, she was built for this. She's stable, and she knows how to sail.'

'You built her?'

'Yes. Listen to the wind. Watch the sails and feel the motion of the boat. Think of what we're doing. Queen Charlotte Sound—thirty miles of open water—nothing between us and Japan—and we're crossing it with no engine, harnessing the wind.'

Pressed against Kurt, she felt only the firm smoothness of his muscles as they surged ahead on the gust.

'Better now?' he asked.

'Yes, thank you. I made a fool of myself, didn't I?'

'Not that I noticed. Think you can stand on your own now?'

'Yes. Yes, of course.'

She saw something flash in the depths of his blue eyes, then his arm fell away from her.

'Here's your coffee!' Andy announced, throwing back the door and handing two mugs out. 'And you'd better appreciate it. The basket went flying down there—threw wet coffee grounds all over—what a mess!'

'You cleaned it up?'

'Oh, yes, brother! I cleaned it up!'

Dana couldn't totally dispel her nervousness, but as time went on, she became more accustomed to the heel. This crazy sensation was something she had never felt before outside of a circus ride. But Kurt was right. It was better to see what was happening, to stay outside.

She curled in the corner of the cockpit, sipping her coffee, talking and laughing with Andy as if she were a seasoned sailor, earning a smile of approval from Kurt.

When their coffee was done, Kurt got up to go back into the cabin. Dana started to follow him.

'Don't get up, Dana. Relax and enjoy it. Your first lesson in sailing.'

She didn't feel nearly as confident with him gone, but she could hardly spend the trip clinging to his shirt tails. She deliberately forced herself to ignore her nervousness, staying above, watching the foaming water, talking to Andy.

By evening, Wendy's tranquilliser had worn off and she proved that she could cook. Supper was served shortly after they turned into the long channel that led to Pruth Bay. Once they entered the channel, they lost all wind. Kurt and Andy furled sails. Dana helped, learning while she got in the way.

Supper was more than delicious—a succulent clam chowder made from shellfish they had collected from the beach the night before, followed by grilled halibut steaks, scalloped potatoes and green salad. Kurt, on watch, had his dinner in the cockpit while the rest of them ate around the dinette table.

Andy was the dishwasher, clearing and washing with a speed that couldn't possibly have been efficient. Then, after they anchored, they went to the beach.

If there was another beach like this in the world, it probably had a thousand or more people spread out on its beautiful, hard-packed sand. Here, the five of them were alone, looking out to the open Pacific over the rocky islands scattered in the bay.

Wayne spread out a blanket for Wendy and they sank down together on the sand, content to relax and enjoy the view. Andy dropped down beside Wayne on the blanket, earning himself a glare from Wendy.

'I want to pick your brains, Wayne. That computer science course I've elected to take this fall—I need to know something about it.'

Dana rolled up her jeans and walked down to the water's edge where Kurt had started a slow, beach-combing trek. She walked along the very edge of the water. The huge rollers swamped her ankles, sweeping the sand away from under her feet.

Above her, Kurt walked slowly, keeping pace with her but staying dry. After a while, she moved up the beach to join him.

'How are your ankles? Hurting from the cold yet?'

'It's lovely! I was here years ago, with my father. I ran out into the waves, swimming.'

'Would you like to try it now?'

'I don't think so.' She had been ten years old, with youth's immunity to cold water. 'Even in summer, this water isn't really warm. Tell me about your boat, Kurt. When did you start building it? How long did it take?'

Kurt bent down to pick up something that glimmered orange in the sand. 'I started her three years ago.' He let the piece of orange flotsam drop back to the beach.

'Where?'

'Halifax.'

'You do get around, don't you? Tell me about it. It must have been a tremendously big job.'

'I didn't do it alone. I was working on this system at

the same time. A lot of the work was done by other hands.'

But he had supervised it all, made sure the vessel was exactly as he wanted. A year ago, when she was complete, *Windflower II* had been launched in the Atlantic; then Kurt had provisioned her and sailed her to the West Indies, through Panama and up to Vancouver.

'I sailed in stages. I had to fly back to Montreal now and again—business. I had a Montreal manufacturer producing the propeller under licence, but it didn't completely free me.'

'You didn't sail all that way alone?'

'Andy joined me when he had holidays, and I picked up a fellow in Panama—he'd been shipwrecked and needed a way home. He sailed as far as San Francisco with me. But mostly I singlehanded her—she's easy to sail.'

She looked out over the water. Not a sign of another ship as far as she could see. 'Alone on a big ocean. Wasn't it lonely?'

'Sometimes.' His blue eyes turned almost black as he stared down at her. 'Yes. Sometimes. But——' He shrugged and turned away to move up the beach.

Dana ran a couple of steps, then matched her stride to his, keeping pace. 'Tell me where else you've sailed.'

'Are you catching the sailing bug? A few hours ago you'd have given anything to be on dry land.'

The waves crashed on the shore, each one surging past the last, sucking up the sand and carrying it higher up the beach. In the sky, the high, white clouds were taking on a tinge of red as the sun approached the horizon.

'Maybe I am. Tell me,' she urged. 'Tell me where you sailed your first boat? The one in the article—Dad read an article about you years ago, It was you, wasn't it?'

'That *was* years ago! Here's Andy—did you and Wayne get your university programme straightened out?'

'Pretty well. Are you trying to get Kurt to tell sailing stories, Dana? He never seems to tell it all. He sailed *Windflower*—the first *Windflower*, that is—in the Atlantic. The Caribbean, Bermuda——'

'Yes,' Kurt agreed, the planes of his face suddenly bleak and hard. 'Bermuda. That was a long time ago.'

'You survived the Bermuda Triangle,' joked Dana, but no one laughed and Dana fell silent, not knowing why Kurt's face was suddenly all bleak lines.

Back on board, Kurt challenged Wayne to a game of chess. They played long and silently, finally arriving at a stalemate.

'Another game?' asked Kurt, and Dana realised that his intense play was his way of escaping from whatever memory she had stirred back on the beach.

'Not me.' Wayne yawned. 'One like that is enough to last me the night.'

'Andy?'

'No way, big brother. You'll slaughter me. The taste of defeat does not appeal to me.'

'Coward!'

'I don't play,' Wendy announced. 'And I'm going to bed.'

'I'll play.' Dana put her book aside. 'I'm a bit rusty, but I'd like a game.'

'I'll go easy on you,' said Kurt, but in fact he played hard, almost as if he couldn't relax even though he wanted to.

'You said you'd go easy,' she accused him. 'You waged war! I didn't have a chance—I don't even know how you did it!'

'Do you want a lesson?'

'All right.' Wayne and Wendy had disappeared.

Andy was lounging on the settee, headphones over his ears, eyes closed.

'Punk rock,' Kurt explained, his eyes following hers. 'I can't handle much of that, so I installed headphones for him.'

'I'm glad.'

They set up the pieces and he showed her why she'd lost. Then they played another game.

She lost.

'Do you know how to go easy in this game?'

'I could let you win,' he offered, grinning.

'Somehow I doubt that. If we're going to do this often, you'd better teach me how to play a better game. But not tonight. Tonight I've had all I can take.'

'Tomorrow,' he promised.

'And if I don't beat you, at least I'll make you work for your victory.'

'You did that tonight. See the furrows in my brow?' The deep lines across his forehead hadn't been caused by her, but she reached a hand up, smoothing one crease gently with her finger.

'Did I do that? Sorry.'

He laughed, but her fingers came away tingling from the feel of his cool skin. Later, in her cabin, she was still rubbing her finger. And smiling. Because he was a nice man. And she liked him.

Would she ever know him well enough to ask what had brought the sadness to his eyes tonight?

The next morning was Dana's first day as cook. She got up early and made coffee for everyone. Wendy staggered in and poured herself a cup.

'Are you all right?' asked Dana.

Wendy stumbled over to the dinette and sat down, turning heavy-lidded eyes on her. 'Coffee'll help. Sleeping pill's not worn off yet.'

Tranquillisers yesterday, sleeping pills last night.

Did Wendy do this all the time? 'Bacon and eggs?' Dana asked. 'How does that sound for breakfast?'

Kurt emerged from the corridor, his hair still damp from the shower she had heard him taking. She poured him a cup of coffee, stirring sugar and cream into it.

'Thanks, Dana. You're looking chipper this morning. Don't start cooking bacon and eggs. We'll have cold cereal for breakfast. You need a chance to find your way around the galley.'

He reached into a cupboard and lifted out a box of Rice Krispies, placing it in front of Wendy. 'Want a bowl, Wendy?'

Wendy made a sour face and pushed the box away.

'I'll try to make lunch more exciting,' Dana promised.

'Keep it simple,' advised Kurt. 'We're sailing, so your galley will be tilted. Don't try anything complicated till you've got the hang of it.' He stepped aside to make room for Wayne and Andy, slipping an arm around Dana's waist as he came close to her. 'Sit down and have breakfast yourself,' he ordered her with a smile. 'You'll get into the work soon enough.'

'I have to get out milk for the cereal,' she protested. He reached a swift hand into the fridge and brought out a quart of milk.

'Fresh milk. Fresh from the freezer, that is. There may still be a chunk of ice floating in it.'

'And sugar——'

He had it in his hand already. 'And the bowls. Now sit down.' He gave her a gentle push and she landed up sitting beside Andy, laughing until she looked up into Andy's eyes and surprised his dark, almost angry gaze on her.

'Peanut butter sandwiches for lunch, I suppose,' grumbled Wendy. 'Are we going to sail this morning?' Kurt nodded. 'That's it for me, then. Goodbye, everybody. I'm going back to my cabin.'

Dana watched her go along the passageway. 'She doesn't look well.'

'She'll get over it,' Wayne sounded bored, but when she met his eyes, they seemed—like Andy's—more angry than anything else. She realised then that Wayne hadn't said good morning to his wife, or goodbye now that she was leaving.

Was everyone grouchy this morning?

Not Kurt. He seemed to be invariably good-humoured.

Kurt and Andy ate quickly, leaving Wayne to do the dishes while they got the vessel under way.

'Are you ready to sail again, Dana?' Kurt called down as they started away from the anchorage with the motor running.

'I think so. Why not? I survived yesterday, didn't I?'

'It won't be as rough today. We're in protected waters now. But remember, we might heel over at any moment—watch where you put things. That kerosene stove——'

'I know. Wendy showed me how to light it. I lit it this morning for coffee.'

'If you have any trouble with it, give a shout.'

'I will.'

Kurt was probably right. She shouldn't try to make anything fancy for lunch. First she had to learn how to cook afloat. She found frozen hamburger patties in the freezer. She would fry the patties and serve them with the fresh buns they'd bought in Port Hardy. And sliced tomatoes and onions. It might not be gourmet, but the hungry men up above would like it.

Kurt would like it. This morning, when he had smiled down at her, his arm around her waist, she had felt they were the only two people in the world. She'd thought he felt something, too, as he looked down into her eyes.

The motion of the vessel was easy today. Dana pushed her head up through the open hatch to the the cockpit to look around. They might be in paradise—blue skies, the sun blazing down; the sails were up, moving them gently through the water. Dana could hardly feel any wind on her face. Kurt was alone in the cockpit. Up front, she could see Andy doing something with rope.

'Are you sure you didn't get lost?' she asked Kurt. 'All this blue sky and sunshine—we could be in the tropics!'

'Could be. I've been watching for the palm trees, but I haven't seen any yet. No sharks either.'

'I'll pass on the sharks, I was just going to start lunch. Hamburgers. How does that sound?'

'Good, but how about more coffee first?'

'Whatever you want, Captain.'

He followed her down below.

'Where's Wayne?' The door to Wendy's cabin was closed, but she didn't think Wayne was in there.

'In the back, working on the computer.'

Dana took out the small container of methyl hydrate and carefully squirted some into the cup below the kerosene burner. She struck a match and the blue flames licked up around the burner. She looked up to find Kurt staring at her.

'Why don't you use propane, Kurt? Most of the fishermen have propane stoves. It's a lot handier.'

'And more explosive. Propane's dangerous on a boat. The gas is heavier than air, it can sink down into the bilge and lie there. Then all it takes is a spark for it to explode.'

He was strangely serious as he lectured her on the virtues of kerosene. 'Kerosene's safer. It won't ignite with just a spark. It needs a wick to burn, or the alcohol primer to bring it up to temperature. Your primer's just burned off. Turn the kerosene on now.' He reached across her and turned it for her. 'If you lose pressure, pump the stove—about ten pumps is usually enough.'

Long after Kurt had returned up on deck, Andy shouted down, 'When's that coffee coming?'

'Soon!'

It seemed to her that the flame had been much higher and hotter this morning. If she pumped up the pressure, the water would surely boil more quickly.

The little pump was in front of the stove. She started pumping it; sliding it out, then pushing it in against the pressure in the tank. Ten pumps.

The flame still seemed low. She kept on pumping, watching the flame, expecting it to come higher.

There was a sudden, explosive hiss, and she jumped back, startled, yelping as the flames suddenly roared up around the stove.

Fire spread everywhere at once. Flames licked up the metal surface behind the stove, across the ceiling. Dana frozen, staring blindly for a moment, then turning with panic to the sink.

Everything was flames. She grasped the tap and turned it on, filling a cup with water.

No. Not water. Water and kerosene—you didn't put water on a grease fire. This was kerosene. The flames were everywhere. Should she——

Then she remembered the fire extinguisher on the wall, found her hands fighting to free it before she realised there was a metal clasp holding it to the wall.

'Get back!' Rough hands pulled her away, flung her against the dinette table. 'Get out of here!'

Kurt threw the catch open and had the extinguisher off the wall. Dana lay against the dinette table, frozen, watching as he played a white spray on the ceiling, then down. The white billowed into clouds against the galley wall.

The fire was gone. Surely there were no flames left yet Kurt continued to play the white cloud from the extinguisher on to the stove, almost as if he couldn't see the fire was out. Finally, the extinguisher was empty. He turned and set it on the counter with a thud.

'I told you to get the hell out of here!' he exploded when he saw she was still standing in the dinette.

'It's out,' she told him. 'The fire's out.' She was starting to shake, but she couldn't look away from Kurt's eyes. The blue had turned deep, almost black as he stared at her.

'Do you have any idea how close——' He stopped abruptly, as if he'd just realised he was shouting.

'Hey, what's going on down there?' called Andy as he erupted into the passageway from above. 'What's all the shouting? Kurt—my God! What a mess,' Andy stopped and surveyed the galley, now covered with a thick layer of white powder.

Kurt's hands gripped Dana's shoulders painfully. He was staring down at her, his voice rough. 'You could have killed yourself! Don't you realise——' One of his hands caught in her hair and he twisted a long tendril around his fingers, staring as though mesmerised.

'Kurt?—Ouch! That hurts.'

'If anything like that happens again, get out! Don't stand here, waiting to be——' His hands clenched in her hair.

'You're hurting me, Kurt. My hair!'

He stared at his hands, then the fingers loosened their grip on her, dropping away. She thought his hands trembled against her neck. Then he turned and pushed his way past Andy.

Andy picked up the fire extinguisher. 'What the hell——?'

'I was cooking——' Dana's voice quavered. She cleared her throat. 'I was pumping the stove, then—it just seemed to explode.'

'You sure made one hell of a mess! First time I've ever seen the after-effects of using one of those fire extinguishers.'

'I'm sorry.'

Andy shrugged. 'Scared the hell out of yourself, I imagine.'

'Kurt was——' He had been more than angry. That had frightened her almost as much as the sudden, raging flames. Kurt, who had seemed so even, so controlled, suddenly looking so furious, then, as he turned away, so bleak.

'Kurt's fanatical about fires,' Andy explained.

'Why? Why is he——?'

'Because of Celeste, my sister. She was asleep, she and her baby alone in the house. There was a fire. They both died. Kurt got there—too late. He helped the firemen, after——'

Dana shuddered, picturing the scene Andy decribed too clearly. Kurt, too late to rescue his sister and nephew.

'I'm sorry. I didn't know.'

'She was beautiful—tall, black hair, long black hair—as long as yours.'

It was hurting Andy, too, remembering. There was nothing she could say to help his feeling of loss. 'I'd better start cleaning up, hadn't I?' she said.

'And I'd better get back on duty. I'm at the wheel. Actually, Otto's steering, but I'd better watch where he's going.'

Otto? Dana was about to ask, then she realised that Otto was—naturally—the autopilot.

She poured the water she had been heating into the sink and added cold water and soap. Coffee would have to wait. She wasn't about to light the stove again yet.

The stove was covered with the white powder.

Around it, everything seemed to be black. She started trying to clean the sooty black coating over the walls and ceiling.

The flames had been everywhere, licking even against the ceiling, but there was little real damage. The wall behind the stove was covered with a sheet of stainless steel. The black washed off the metal with cleanser and warm water.

Not the ceiling. It didn't seem to be actually burned but the white paint was black and dirty-looking no matter how hard she scrubbed. Her water was turning black, but the ceiling was far from white.

'You'll need more water.' Kurt was back, frowning at the ceiling.

'I don't think it'll come clean even then. I'm sorry.'

'We'll paint it. Now, tell me how the fire started.'

'I was pumping the stove. The flame was low. I turned it right up, but—so I pumped it. Then suddenly there was a hiss—kind of an explosive hiss, and——'

'How many times did you pump?'

'You said ten, and I did that, but it didn't seem to make any difference. So I kept pumping, trying to——' She shrugged helplessly. 'I don't know how many times.'

'The burner must have been plugged. Perhaps a bit of dirt in the kerosene clogged it. You must have kept pumping a long time. The pressure-release valve finally let go.'

He showed her the valve at the back of the stove. 'It must have sprayed kerosene when it blasted off. That's what the flames were. Nothing actually burned except the kerosene.'

'I'm sorry. It was my fault.' She would feel better if he would smile, if his eyes would show some sign of warmth.

'I'll clean the burner for you.' He disassembled the

stove and cleaned it while Dana drained her dirty water and replaced it with cold, soapy water.

They worked together, silently. 'You don't need to help me,' Dana protested once, guilty because this was her fault, her mess. He said nothing, but lifted a stack of cups out of their holder and handed them to her for washing. Everything, everywhere, was covered with the white powder.

Andy came down once, looking around at the mess and asking, 'Any coffee yet?'

'Make your own if you want coffee,' Kurt told him. Andy shrugged and disappeared above.

Wayne came forward and blinked, staring around. 'What happened?'

'A fire,' Dana told him. Kurt wasn't volunteering any more information, so she went on. 'A small fire.' It hadn't seemed small at the time, but the flames hadn't damaged anything except the paint on the ceiling. 'I was pumping the stove. I pumped too much and the pressure-release valve gave way.'

Wayne picked up a glass from the open cupboard on the wall. 'You'll want to wash these, too. They're coated with powder.'

That was most of the damage. White powder on the dishes, the food, the pots and pans. White powder on the floor, the diesel stove, the chimney. White powder even inside the closed cupboards in the galley—how had it got in there?

'I think I'll replace those extinguishers with Halon,' Kurt told Wayne. 'This powder makes one hell of a mess!'

'Quite a mess, isn't it? Do you need any help with this clean-up?'

Kurt shook his head. 'Any more people in here and we'll just be stumbling over each other. Before you go, Wayne, dig in the fridge and get us all a Coke. Take one out to Andy, too.'

The Coke tasted good. 'Wash away some of the baking soda in our throats,' said Kurt, drinking down half of his in a long swallow.

'Is that what's in those extinguishers? Baking soda?'

'Right. Not toxic, but it can sure make a mess, can't it?'

She nodded. 'Kurt, I'm——'

'Don't apologise again, for goodness' sake. If it was anyone's fault, it was mine. I shouldn't have let you use that stove until you knew more about it, and I could have done a better job of fireproofing this galley. I thought I had, but I never thought of the kerosene blowing off the valve and catching like that. I certainly never prepared for the flames getting up as high as the ceiling. I'll make damned sure is doesn't happen again.'

While Dana finished the clean-up—actually, it wasn't finished, for days, everyone found white powder in places that they'd never thought of when they were cleaning up—Kurt went to work on the stove enclosure. From somewhere he produced a sheet of gleaming stainless steel which he cut and bent into an extension of the fire wall around the stove.

'Put the hamburgers back into the freezer,' he told Dana when she started wondering what to do about lunch. 'Make us sandwiches. Open a can of something to spread on bread. There's some salmon in that cupboard under the dinette.'

She didn't argue. She still wasn't ready to light the stove again.

CHAPTER THREE

THE next night they anchored in a large bay a few miles before Milbanke Sound, the second stretch of open water they would cross.

They had had a wild ride on the wind in Seaforth Channel, then burst into the sudden shelter of the harbour, drifting almost silently on the rippled water.

'Ideal for dinghy sailing,' Kurt decided as he looked around at their anchorage. 'Andy, would you lower the dinghy and rig it for sailing. I'm going to teach Dana to sail.'

'I'll take her,' volunteered Andy. 'You're the cook.'

'I'll do it. Supper's under control. The roast and vegetables are in the oven—call me on the loudhailer if they start to burn.'

Kurt went below and set the table while Andy rigged the dinghy. 'There,' he pronounced as he put the salt and pepper on the table. 'It's all ready except for serving. Are you ready, Dana? Don't wear anything that can't get wet.'

'Are we going to get wet?'

'We might, but we'll be wearing life jackets. If we do happen to take some water aboard, it won't matter.'

They sat together in the back of the dinghy, close by necessity. 'There's no heavy keel,' he told her, 'only a centreboard. In a dinghy, the sailor provides balance with his own weight.'

The wind was light with an occasional brisk gust. They played with it, drifting along, then tacking and coming back fast into the wind. Kurt handled the tiller at first, then he turned it over to Dana as they drifted gently downwind.

'Now bring it around,' he urged her, his voice low in her ear.

She pushed the rudder over hard. The boat swerved, the sail flapping wildly until she pulled the line in to tighten it. They started to sail faster as the dinghy headed up into the wind, the sail still flapping slightly. She pulled the line tighter and they heeled sharply. Dana and Kurt leaned out to the side to balance. Caught by the excitement of the rushing water, she pulled harder still on the line. They raced along, the water almost at the top of the little boat on the downward side.

'Pull it in more. I dare you.'

'I'm a sucker for a dare.' She pulled. The water skimmed along the edges of the boat, splashing against their feet.

'How's that?' she shouted. The wind tried to carry her words away.

'You'll do.' He didn't have to shout; his lips were next to her ear, his arm curved around her back as he braced himself to lean out, balancing the dinghy. She was wedged in the curve of his arm.

All too soon, she heard Andy's voice boom over the loudhailer, filling the deserted bay.

'Your roast is done, Kurt. Come and get it before we eat it all!'

'Bring the tiller around,' Kurt instructed her, explaining how she should dock.

'Very good,' Andy complimented her, grasping the mast of their little craft to keep it alongside while Kurt sorted out the painter. 'You did a really nice job of that.' His eyes were warm with admiration. She was flattered, but in the days that followed she began to wonder if Andy's growing infatuation with her was going to become a problem.

Sailing the dinghy helped Dana to lose her fear of sailing. In a brisk wind, she would go on deck, watching the wild surge of water as they drove hard and fast into the waves. Down below, working on the articles in her cabin, she was always aware of movement, the vessel's constant response to wind and water.

When she had finished the first magazine article, Kurt made a special trip to the nearest Indian village to mail it along with her roll of film, leaving Dana on tenterhooks, waiting for word from the editor.

Further north, they stopped to visit Butedale—the remains of what had once been a flourishing cannery town of several hundred people. When the cannery closed, the town had deteriorated, been abandoned except for a watchman and his family. Finally, the ghost town was sold, along with an incredible hydroelectric plant driven by an abundant stream flowing down the mountainside.

Since the sale, some of the old buildings had been reclaimed, some of the floats torn out and others repaired. Butedale had reopened, but this time as a general store, marina and motel set on the edge of the ruins.

Kurt took pictures with her camera while she talked with the managers, then they explored the ruins together while Wayne and Andy hiked up the mountain for a look at the lake, promising the manager they would keep a sharp lookout for bears.

Wendy stayed in the general store, drinking coffee and looking through the used books offered for trade.

'Fascinates you, doesn't it?' Kurt handed Dana the camera as they walked back down the ramp to *Windflower II*.

'The ruins,' she mused, looking around at warehouses crumbled to nothing, the remains of pilings where once there had been a large network of floats for the fishing boats. 'Just imagine this place when it was operating. All those houses on the hillside occupied by cannery workers. Who do you think lived in that one? Right over there, above the fence.'

'That must have been the manager's. The local ruler; he'd have to have the largest house—watch your step, Dana. This wharf is slippery—there's a rotten spot! Just to your right.'

'I'm okay. I wonder what he was like? But then there would have been a succession of bosses here, wouldn't there? Some of them were probably real tyrants, and some—it seems so sad, the whole town being shut down. Why? What happened? The fellow in the store said it was the big canneries, but——'

'Ice,' he said shorty.

'Ice?'

'There were small canneries all along the coast at one time. This is one of the more spectacular ruins, but there are others, disintegrated to nothing more than a few pilings. The fishermen fished close to home, brought their catch in to the nearest cannery quickly before the fish could spoil.

'Then, with modern refrigeration, the fishermen started carrying ice in their holds. Ice was available in great quantities at every port. You're from a fishing community; if you think about it, you know what happened. They could fish further, keep their catch longer. They could deliver to larger canneries, further away. Small operations like Butedale couldn't compete. The big canneries bought them out, then closed them down.'

'But I wonder if it was really worth it.'

Kurt took her hand as they reached the bottom of the ramp. 'I know. I can't help wondering, too. Was it really that much more economical overall? To build new plants, displace the workers . . . Or was it just that, like everyone else, the canneries were caught up in the conviction that bigger is better.'

They turned together and looked back up at the hillside. 'At least there's something here again,' Dana said finally. 'The place is alive again.'

'I hope they make a go of it—watch out for that board—I think I got some good pictures. You must have that notebook of yours filled by now. You were talking to the couple in the store for a long time. Have you thought of doing an article just on Butedale? Quite separate from the cruising articles.'

'You must be reading my mind.' She tapped the notebook she always carried tucked in her hip pocket of her jeans. 'I think I've got enough here to make a good general interest article. That, and the ideas in my head—if I get them down before I lose them.'

'Why don't you go off and work on it now, while everything's quiet.'

Dana shut the door to her little cabin. Not to shut out Kurt, but because she knew it would be noisy when the others returned.

She transferred her notes to the computer, working out the framework she had visualised for the article on Butedale, noting down ideas and parts of ideas that seemed clear in her mind now, but would disappear if she didn't record them permanently.

She hardly noticed when they cast off from the floats, though she had to shift her seating when they heeled in response to the sails going up.

'Dana?'

Kurt's voice, his distinctive rap on her door.

'Hmm? Come in.' She typed a few words, finishing the sentence.

'Phone call for you! Radio-telephone. The editor of

the yachting magazine.'

'Well?' demanded Wendy when Dana came out of the aft cabin where the radios were located. 'What did he say?'

Kurt hadn't heard the call. He'd left her alone with the radio, but now he read her smile and said. 'They're taking the article.'

'You are psychic, aren't you? You're right. They're taking the whole series—this article, and five more!'

'We should celebrate,' said Wendy, then, 'if only there were a nightclub. We're in the the middle of nowhere. Kurt, where's the nearest nightclub?'

'Would you accept a hot spring?'

They went north to Bishop Bay where a nearby yacht club had transformed a natural hot spring into a haven for cruising yachtsmen.

Kurt and Dana set crab traps before they docked, then they all collected bathing suits and towels, climbing over the rocks to the bathhouse. Together, they soaked in the enclosed hot pool, listening to the noise of the forest as they let the hot water wash over them.

Back at the yacht, Wendy and Dana prepared a spread of snack food for the party. Andy dug in the hold for wine while Kurt steamed the crab they had trapped. When the whole feast was spread out on the coach-house roof, they sat listening to soft music playing on the stereo below, sipping wine, eating crab and crackers—quickly demolishing the one crab they had caught.

Dana watched the wine swirl in her class, the red sunset streaking across the glimmering water. She reached for a piece of crab and found the plate empty. 'Oysters,' she pondered. 'Wouldn't oysters be lovely?'

'You can't get oysters in these waters,' said Andy.

'Not without a can opener,' agreed Kurt, on his feet

and heading below.

'You're not really going to eat those things?' protested Wendy when Kurt reappeared with a freshly opened tin of smoked oysters and two forks. 'Have you ever really looked at an oyster?'

Dana shared a deliciously secret smile with Kurt. 'Don't look, Dana,' he said. 'Just close your eyes and enjoy them. Don't let these heathens spoil a good oyster.'

It was Wendy who started the dancing, turning up the stereo and dragging Wayne to his feet, moving slowly with him on the deck. As the last bars of the music faded, she slipped away from her husband, putting her hand out to Kurt.

'Dance with me, Kurt!' she demanded.

Kurt let himself be pulled to his feet, dancing with a smoothness that might have been impressive if he had had more room than the deck. Wayne turned to Dana, holding her awkwardly as they danced, unaccustomed to a tall woman in his arms. To cover his nervousness, he talked computers.

When the dance was over, Dana turned to Kurt. It was her turn now. But Andy appeared at Wayne's elbow, his arms ready for Dana, sighing dramatically as they started to dance. And Kurt just shrugged, joking that he wasn't going to try to compete with youth.

Andy's young arms held her too close. When the tempo picked up, Dana slipped away and danced to the music herself, facing Andy, out of reach.

It turned into a wild dance, Dana's hair shimmering in the moonlight as she moved to the music. Once, as the tempo slowed momentarily, she found Kurt's eyes on her, dark and mysterious.

She tumbled into the deckchair next to him, laughing and exhausted.

'Dance with me, Kurt.' He looked down at her,

'You're miles away. Come and dance.'

'You've had enough. Sit down and relax.'

'Later? Will you dance with me later?'

When he did, she moved gracefully into his arms. It was where she belonged, she realised with only a slight sense of surprise.

She had done this in dreams, his arm at her back. In her dreams, he had held her tight against him, so that her full breasts were crushed by his muscular chest. In dreams, his eyes looked deep into hers, telling her he loved her.

'Enjoying your party?' he asked.

'It's lovely. Thank you.'

'You've done well. A six-part series—that's quite an accomplishment.'

'It'll be good for your sales, too, Kurt.' He steered her clear of the anchor on the foredeck.

'I know. It takes time to build up sales for a new product. Those articles will give it a head start. You've more than justified your passage. I should be paying you a salary!'

'No, of course you shouldn't. I'm being paid for the articles.' Dana closed her eyes, enjoying having his arms around her.

Later, in her bunk, she fell asleep with the memory of that dance. One day, she told herself sleepily, there would be more than a dance. Tonight, if they had been alone, she thought he might have kissed her.

In the middle of the night, she came wide awake and alert. She lay, her eyes wide open to the dark, listening to a faint squeaking sound for some time before she identified it.

Outside, in the channel, another boat must have gone by setting up a wake that rocked them at their dock, sending the fenders squeaking as they rubbed between the boat and the wharf.

She slipped out of her blankets, not bothering to put on a robe. Her filmy gown was more than enough in the warm night.

Outside, on deck, the night was magical. She walked softly, in bare feet, standing at the side rail, looking out over the water.

The trees rose to mountains around her, surrounding the bay. The moon shone faintly from behind a cloud, outlining the mountains against the sky, the water against the land. A night bird hooted softly, sharing the darkness with her.

Kurt had closed the cabin door and climbed into his sleeping bag. He had had too much of the wine. He'd been sitting, talking, watching Dana dance. Then some trick of lighting had changed her golden hair to a dark cloud around her head and he had been caught up in the past again, remembering things best left forgotten.

Sleep now. In the morning he would wash away memories with another trip to the hot spring, then start moving, escape this haunting loneliness.

He fell into a half sleep where he wandered between today and yesterday.

Celeste. Walking along the beach in Bermuda, her long dark hair swinging on her back, long shapely legs below. She had been walking away when he first saw her, a tantalising stranger.

The next day he followed her when she went swimming, striking up a conversation on the diving platform.

She had dropped her eyes, strangely shy. When she looked up, her dark eyes met his with a quickly concealed flash that told him she was interested, too.

He had to pursue her carefully, his shy young love, wooing her with a gentleness that was strange to him after years of wandering the world and finding his pleasures in some of the rougher places.

He knew she was attracted by the romance of his life-style. The men she had been carefully introduced to by her parents had not been wanderers, travelling the world in a sailboat, living off the ocean. She had called him her blond god from the seas, had let him claim every one of her days, moving closer until he had her in his arms.

He might have had stiff opposition from her parents, but the success of the propeller he had developed gave him enough conventional respectability to satisfy Celeste's mother. Andy, her father, had never tried to oppose Kurt. Instead, he helped him, giving legal advice on patent applications, putting him in touch with a Montreal manufacturer that could give Kurt's inventions a wider distribution.

Through all the business dealings, there was Celeste on the beach, Celeste in a daring, frothy dancing dress that was cut low between her small breasts, Celeste letting him put his arms around her, kiss her, touch her.

He had been alone so many years when he met her. Their love was like a salvation, returning him to humanity. He had taken her sailing, but sailing had frightened her and they hadn't repeated the experience.

Their wedding, Celeste in another filmy gown, waiting for him, frightened and virginal . . . growing large with his child, the tiny girl she had given birth to in the second year of their marriage.

They had settled in Montreal. He had taken up the role of young entrepreneur, developing a whole series of products that were patented and cleverly distributed by the manufacturers Andy had found for him. He bought Celeste a house. His sun-bleached hair grew darker, his skin lighter. Too many evenings he worked late, but when he stayed home the nights were magical. Talking on the patio, making plans, watching little Patricia grow.

The baby fascinated him. She had Celeste's dark hair and the deep blue eyes she had inherited from Kurt. He would stand, watching her sleep with the dark lashes fanned over her baby face, waiting for her eyes to open to reveal the sea-blue gaze. Sometimes he watched until Celeste touched his arm, urging him away, then they would shut the door softly on Patricia and go into their own room.

Touching her, loving her.

In the darkness, rocking softly, Kurt felt the magic again. In dreams, he held his wife in his arms.

Awakening, lying in his lonely bunk, he found his arms empty, knew he would never hold her again.

He slept again, fitfully. Hours later, he opened his eyes, reaching for Celeste and finding her gone.

Sometimes, in the night, she woke and went to check on Patricia. Still half in the dream, he slipped out of his bed. He didn't feel the coolness on his bare skin as he came out on the deck.

He couldn't see the trees or the water. He saw only Celeste. There was hardly any light, but he could see her tall form, the silhouette of her long dark hair, the vague outline of one of these filmy nightgowns she liked to wear.

She was standing, waiting for him. Still shy after their years of marriage, she would not come to him; but when he moved to her, touched her, she would slide her arms around his neck, receiving him. She was waiting for him in the dark, waiting for them to love together.

He moved slowly, silently, towards her.

Dana had felt the gentle shifting of the deck under her feet, realised that someone had woken below. Then she heard the hatch slide open.

The night was too dark for her to see his face or even

identify the colour of his hair, but she knew at once that
it was Kurt.

He was so silent, moving so slowly, just a form in the
dark. He said nothing and she held wordless, waiting
for him to come closer.

She moved one step towards him, then stopped, her
nightgown drifting around her, her hair moving on her
shoulders.

He stared silently at her. The clouds had moved
steadily across the sky, leaving only the faintest hint of
light from the stars.

'I knew you'd be here.' His voice was husky, almost
unrecognisable. 'When I woke and you were gone, I
knew you'd be here.' He just touched her hair with one
hand, brushing it away from her face, drawing it
tickling along her bare shoulder.

Dana stood, not daring to move.

Both his hands were on her face now. He looked
down, as if he could see the fullness of her breasts where
the gown parted.

'Were you waiting for me?' His voice was even
lower, ragged with some emotion that frightened her
for a moment.

'Yes,' she whispered. Hadn't she always been
waiting for him?

His hands moved to her shoulders, sliding along the
silky fabric, a soft caress that made her gasp. He bent
and brushed his lips gently against the side of her
mouth, making her lips open to him, not taking her lips,
but teasing, brushing each nerve ending of her face
with his lips until she could bear it no longer and her
arms went up, lacing though his hair as they had always
wanted to, drawing him down so that his lips met hers
and took hers.

He raised his head, his unsteady breathing echoing
her own. He said nothing, just looked at her through the

darkness, then bent again to reclaim her lips.

She opened her lips to him again, needing the touch of his tongue on the inside of her upper lip, the feel of his hair sliding through her fingers as she gripped it, arching so that she came against him until she felt, rather than heard, his gasp of pleasure.

'You're different tonight,' he told her in low, husky voice. His hands softly rubbed the fabric against her back, dropped to her waist, slipping up the front of her gown until they cupped her heavy breasts, lifting them so that they rested against his palms, the nipples touching his bare chest through the thin fabric of her gown. His mouth took hers then, and she answered his passion, quivering in anticipation when his hands moved again, knowing the touch of them before she felt it, her body melting in surrender as he brushed the sensitive places, moving his mouth away from hers and bending to trail fire along her soft skin.

'I need you,' he whispered, feeling her own need of him as he never had before.

He slid the fabric down from her shoulders, slowly, watching in the darkness as if he could see her warm female curves springing free. His hands stroked softly over her skin, tracing the shape of her.

'Kurt?' she whispered. His hands slid behind her again, pulling her hips against him so that she could feel his own desperate need of her. His mouth moved on her lips and she returned his kiss with a passion she was learning from his touch. She slipped her arms free of the gown and pulled his head down to her, holding it with trembling fingers laced through his hair as his lips moved down to press warm kisses along her neck, then down again on to the soft, sensitive mounds that seemed to ache for his touch.

He groaned against her hot skin. She answered his caress with her hands, moving softly on his skin to tell him how she ached for him.

'It's been so long. I've missed you so, Celeste.'

Dana's hands froze, her body turning cold with shock. She pushed against him. His lips left her skin and she was standing in his arms, her nightgown insecurely hanging on her hips, feeling nothing but the horrifying certainty that he had said what she thought she had heard.

'Kurt?' Her voice was sharp and clear, without the husky tones of passion. The moon worked its way clear of a cloud and bathed them in light. She saw the flush of passion leaving his face pale and bleak as his eyes cleared. She knew the moment when he recognised her.

'Who did you think I was? Whom were you making love to?'

The moon bathed her nakedness with soft light. Feeling his eyes on her, she moved her hands, reaching down, about to cover herself, draw the gown up over her body to hide from him.

Then she stopped, letting her hands drop to her sides again, standing still and straight brfore him.

She wanted him to remember her as she was. Not as Celeste.

'Dana?' He shook his head, clearing the dreams away. 'My God! I——' He gestured blindly, turned away from her, ran his hands through his hair, seeing what he had not seen a few moments ago—the water. The trees.

The woman, her body fuller than Celeste's, her skin fairer. 'Dana—I'm sorry. I didn't——'

She crossed the deck to him, her gown once more covering her. She touched him, wincing as he jerked away, then suddenly angry.

'Who's Celeste?' she asked, knowing the answer.

'My wife.'

Kurt's wife. Andy's sister.

'Do you—do I look like her?'

'You don't look anything like her.'

'But tonight—just a few seconds ago, you thought I was her.'

'It was dark. I was half asleep, dreaming. I forgot—I thought—I don't know. Maybe the wine—dammit, Dana, I'm making excuses. But I woke up, forgetting somehow that she—when I came up here, in the dark, Celeste was standing there, waiting for me. She had long, dark hair. She was tall. She always liked to wear that kind of gown—frothy, filmy. We used to . . . She's dead,' he ended flatly.

'In the dark? I look like her in the dark?'

'Yes.'

'Then we'd better keep the lights on, hadn't we?'

'Dana——' She was moving away from him. He felt a sudden, unwilling awareness of her. A tall, blonde woman, surprisingly voluptuous under that gown. Walking away. 'Dana! I——'

She didn't turn back, kept walking.

Kurt followed silently through the companionway, watched her walk to her cabin and close the door behind her.

Was there anything in the etiquette books about apologising to a woman for imagining she was someone else?

CHAPTER FOUR

'ALASKA,' breathed Dana. 'Would you believe that we're actually in Alaska?'

Kurt spun the wheel. He didn't look at her, hadn't looked at her in many days. 'Give Andy a hand with the anchor, Dana.'

He had been turning away, pushing her away, ever since they left Bishop Bay. When she had asked if she could take a watch and learn to navigate, Kurt had put her on watch with Andy, assigned Andy to teach her pilotage.

When Dana sailed the dinghy, she sailed it alone, or with Andy.

He had even stopped playing chess with her.

Dana stepped on to the deck, careful not to trip over Wendy where she was spread out over the deck, her legs glistening with suntan oil, her face hidden by a towel—protection from the hot sun. Dana hung on to a wire stay while she swung around Wendy's hidden head, forward to where Andy stood at the bow with the anchor line in his hand.

They were drifting slowly into a bay at the head of a narrow inlet. On either side of the glistening water, green mountains rose sharply out to a clear blue sky. Above, the hot afternoon sun blazed down on them.

'Can I give you a hand, Andy?'

'With what? All I've got to do is to let the anchor go when Kurt says, then tie off when there's enough rode out.'

Kurt called forward, 'Have you spotted the rock?'

'Yes, captain!' Andy shouted back. 'Right over

there!' Kurt picked up a pair of binoculars for a closer
look.

Dana asked Andy, 'Where's the rock?'

'See the kelp patch floating in the water? Right
there. Can't actually see the rock now, but it dries at
low tide, so we sure don't want to anchor on top of it.'

A moment later, Kurt shouted, 'Let it go, Andy!' and
Andy lifted his foot and stood back as some fifty feet of
steel chain flew noisily out over the bow roller. As the
anchor hit bottom, the chain stopped, then began to
pull slowly over the side link by link.

'It's on the bottom!'

'Let out about two hundred feet as I reverse. We
want her well set. It's likely to blow tonight.'

Dana glanced back at Kurt, met his eyes staring back
at her with a shock. They stood motionless for a long
moment, the length of the boat between them, their
eyes touching. Then Kurt looked away. His face
seemed hard and impassive as he stared off at the
shore.

'Have you and Kurt had a fight?' asked Andy
curiously.

'Why?' Dana stalled.

'On a vessel this size, when two of the people on
board are avoiding each other, it shows.'

What would Andy think if she told him the truth?
That Kurt had found her on the deck one night and
made love to her until he discovered that it wasn't his
wife in his arms.

She had only known him a few weeks. He was
attractive, and she was attracted, but it shouldn't be
more than that. When she fell in love, it should be with
a man who was free to love her, not one entangled in
shadows of the past, who turned away whenever their
eyes met.

When the anchor was set, Kurt got out a fishing rod

to jig for bottom fish. His hook hadn't been down more than thirty seconds when it was taken.

'It's a big one,' he grunted as it fought against his attempt to reel in. 'Someone get the gaff. Boy, I don't know——' The rod tip jerked sharply, twice, then the line started going out, fast.

'You're going to lose him!' Dana cried. 'He'll get away.'

'I've still got him. He's just not ready to come in yet.' The line stopped going out and Kurt started working it slowly in, 'I'm not sure I want to see him until he's tired out. He's—there he goes again!'

Watching him, she could see a ten-year-old Kurt, jumping with excitement as he caught his first fish.

Andy leaned out over the safety lines. 'Hey, do you see that sucker! A halibut—a big one! A hundred pounds, at least! Do you want me to work the rod for a while?'

'No way! This is my fish.' Dana saw his jaw clench as he pulled up on the rod. Kurt and the fish waged a brief battle, after which the fish had gained another twenty-five feet of line. 'If I'm going to lose him, I'll lose him on my own.'

'Should I start dinner?' Dana wondered. 'Or should I wait until——?'

'Our dinner is on the other end of this line. Don't even imply that I might not land him! Have you got that gaff ready? Andy, open the gate so I can—oh, you beauty! Look at that—easy, now. Just stay on the hook. Andy, hold the rod. Hold it steady and pass me the gaff. Dana——'

'Yes?'

'Get me the fish bonker, then stand back, for goodness' sakes! I don't think it weighs a hundred pound, but it's big! If it starts flapping around, it can do a lot of damage.'

The fish was just breaking water, the hook caught behind the immense, gaping mouth; the flat, broad halibut hanging down into the water. Then it twitched, curling its powerful muscles and jerking the line hard.

'How are you going to get him on board?' queried Dana.

'I'd like to shoot him first, but——'

'I'll get the .22,' volunteered Andy.

'No, you won't. We're in foreign waters and I haven't a clue what Alaskan laws might be about shooting from a boat,' Kurt slipped the gaff in and jerked it up. 'The bonker, Dana! Quick! Andy, hang on to this while I get down.'

He climbed quickly over the side to stand on the rub rail, hooking an arm around the stanchion. He was almost on a level with the fish now. 'Hold him steady while I try to put him out of action.'

The halibut gave a mighty heave and brought his tail out of the water, then slammed it back, covering Kurt in a spray of water. Kurt shook his head to clear his eyes of hair and water, hanging on hard. After a not-so-brief battle, the fish hung limp on the gaff and Andy and Kurt accepted Wayne's help lifting it on to the deck.

'A hundred pounds,' Andy repeated.

'Seventy, anyway,' Kurt decided. 'What a fish! I had my doubts if we could land it.'

'You should have shot it. Remember *Evening Star?*'

'I was remembering the whole time I was bringing this fish in.' Kurt shook his head, spraying water somewhat like a large, wet dog. 'That's why I wanted the bonker before I got him on board.'

The evening breeze was blowing his wet clothes against his body. He didn't seem to realise that he was wet. 'Dana, have you ever seen what happens when a halibut wages war on a boat?'

She grinned back at him. 'You're going to tell me one

of these fish stories—I won't believe a word of it.'

'This one's true, I swear. Andy and I saw the boat in Victoria. She'd just come in from the west coast of the Island. Her galley and salon were a disaster. The captain and his wife had caught a big halibut—about a seventy-pounder—and somehow managed to land it on deck without killing it first. The fish was flopping around—you saw how energetic they are? Well, it flopped into the cockpit. The companionway was open, and it fell down into the boat.

'Once it got inside, the fish went wild, flinging itself around, breaking up the inside of the boat. Seventy pounds of live halibut is no joke inside a boat! The table was smashed—totally destroyed. Most of the dishes were broken, lanterns broken, books torn to bits, lying on the floor.'

'So you weren't joking about the gun?'

'Not a bit. If we'd been in our own waters, I'd have had Andy get the .22 out. As it was, it went easier than I thought. I——' Kurt broke off, staring at her. 'I was lucky to land him so easily,' he finished on a flat note.

'It's your fish, Kurt. How do you want him cooked?' Her voice was too high, brittle.

'Some steaks off the tail, I guess. It doesn't matter.' He turned away and started gathering the fishing gear together.

Wendy had sat up and was staring at the halibut on the deck. 'You're a fisherman's daughter, Dana. Any good at cleaning and canning fish? It's not my line of country.'

'I can clean the little ones. This one's going to be quite a job—more like skinning a moose! But I can cook him and can him. Kurt, I know you've got a pressure cooker; do you have any jars?'

'Under the bunk in your cabin.' He was busy putting the fishing tackle away so didn't look up.

That evening, Dana worked with Kurt and Andy in the galley, preparing the halibut for canning.

'Big fish,' said Dana as she took a piece from Kurt and placed it in a jar.

He nodded and cut another piece. She shrugged and worked on silently. If he didn't want to talk, they wouldn't talk.

'Boat coming in.' announced Andy as the last traces of light were fading from the sky. 'A big power boat—anchoring to the west of us.'

Kurt drew his filleting knife smoothly under a section of fish bones. 'Good. Row over and ask them if they'd like some halibut. We've got more than we can handle.'

But Andy returned minutes later. 'Would you believe the guy is allergic to halibut? How can anyone be allergic to halibut?'

The canner was just coming up to pressure for the second time. On the counter, several jars of halibut were cooling from the first load.

'We could freeze some of it,' Dana suggested.

Kurt laughed. 'Have you looked in that freezer recently? We stocked up so well the last time we went shopping, I doubt if you'll get more than five pounds of fish in there. I'll just have to keep the canner going.'

'I'll look after it,' Dana offered. 'You and Andy can go to bed if you like.' Wendy had already retired with a book, dragging Wayne along with her. 'After all, it is my day to cook.'

'This is a bit beyond the normal duties of a cook,' Kurt protested. 'I'll look after it.'

'Kurt, I don't mind——'

'Go to bed, Dana. I couldn't sleep, anyway. Not while the stove's still going.'

Dana shrugged and fell silent. How could she fight that? The stove. Fire. Celeste.

'Andy can help me. He never sleeps, anyway.'

As Kurt had predicted earlier, the wind came up sharply in the middle of the night. Dana lay in the darkness of her cabin, listening as the wind came up to drown the hissing of the pressure cooker. She heard the lines starting to slap against the mast, then the sound of footsteps on the deck above. Whoever it was—Kurt or Andy—must have tied the ropes off away from the mast, because the slapping sound stopped.

She could see mountains outlined against a bright moonlit sky through her porthole. A short distance away, the power boat's anchor light made a bright star against the sky.

She knew they were securely anchored, but she found herself lying awake, listening to the wind, riding the motion of the waves that stirred in the night.

The hiss of the pressure cooker stopped for the last time. The lights went out. Dana pushed a pillow into shape and turned on to her stomach.

Too hot. She kicked a blanket off, then reached for it a moment later as the cool air tickled her legs.

Eventually, she slept.

The wind had begun to howl in the rigging when she woke. She felt stifled, hot, despite the wind outside. She reached for a jacket and slipped out through the darkened salon, making her way by the moonlight shining in through the portholes.

The wind on the deck whipped her hair and she caught at it with her hands, pushing it under the collar of her jacket. The deck felt cold against her bare feet.

The moon slipped behind a dark cloud, leaving only a faint light in the bay. The power boat—Dana turned, looking for the point of light on its mast. It had anchored on the west side, surely?

She must have got turned around, lost her sense of direction. The power boat's anchor light was over to their left, quite a distance away. She pushed her hair down again and studied the outline of the shore, trying to get her bearings.

Over there, what looked like the stream coming down from the mountain. The rock would be—about there. And the other boat . . .

She hadn't lost her bearings at all. She was right, and the power boat was in the wrong place.

Kurt was sleeping on his side, turned towards the open door of his cabin. He always left his door open so he could hear in case there was anything he should wake for in the night.

'Kurt,' she whispered.

He didn't move. In the moonlight she could see his head cradled on his arm. His pillow had fallen on to the floor. His blanket was thrown off, the sheet twisted around his hips.

She touched his arm. 'Kurt?'

His hand locked around her wrist, pulling her down towards him. She reached up quickly to switch on his light.

'Kurt, it's Dana.'

He winced against the light, drawing his arm across his eyes. 'Dana? What——?' He sat up, reaching for his jeans. 'What's wrong?' He looked young and vulnerable, blinking.

'That power boat—I think they've dragged anchor. I think they're right over that rock!'

'Get the spotlight. I'll be there in a second.'

The wind was still rising, Out on deck, it whipped cold raindrops against their faces. 'I think you're right, Dana. Let's look at the chart. Get——'

'Right here. I had it out, checking.'

'Good girl.' He gave her arm a quick squeeze as he took the chart from her and bent down by the night light in the cockpit to check it.

'It looks like he's sitting right over the rock. And the tide's going out. By morning he'll be on that rock if we don't do something.'

The wind peaked in a sudden howling gust. Dana shivered as the cold rain hit her skin.

'Are you all right?' He brought her against him with a strong arm. 'You're not dressed for this.'

'Neither are you. How are we going to warn him? You could row over——'

'Not in this wind. Listen to it; it's getting worse. The water's far too rough for a nine-foot dinghy! We'll have to wake him up some other way.'

'You could try calling him on the radio.'

'I don't think he has one. There was no sign of an antenna on the boat. His lights are out. He's probably fast asleep, has no idea that his anchor's dragged all the way across the bay.'

Dana nestled against him and he drew her closer. 'Go and get some warm clothes on, dear. I'll get the spotlight and see if I can get any reaction shining it on his windows.'

She left the warmth of his protective arm and went below for raingear. In Kurt's cabin she found the warm jacket he used on windy days, and a rain slicker.

He had the spotlight plugged in and was playing the beam over the power boat.

'I brought your jacket.' He slipped his arms into it absently and zipped it up.

'Are you warm enough now, Dana?'

She nodded. 'Any sign of life over there?'

'Nothing. I've been shining the light in the portholes, but he's sleeping like a baby. You'd think, with his boat rocking like that in the waves, that he'd sleep lightly.'

'You could blow your horn.'

'In this wind, he wouldn't hear it. I'm going to try shooting off a red flare over him.'

The distress flare shot high over the power boat, bathing the entire bay in an eerie red light as it fell back into the water.

The other boat remained shrouded in darkness except for the anchor light at its mast top.

'It's not going to wake him,' Kurt realised as the red faded. 'No wonder, I suppose. We've got three people down below who've managed to sleep through all this.'

'You could try flashing the search light on and off. If it's shining right into the cabin he's sleeping in, it might wake him.'

'Let's try it. I sure don't want to have to launch that dinghy in this—and I can't pull up anchor and go over there. At this state of the tide, we draw enough that we might just hit that rock. I'll hold the light. You switch it on and off.'

'It's not working,' Dana fretted moments later as the power boat remained dark. 'Maybe it's the wrong porthole,'

Keep it up a while longer.' Kurt shifted to balance the big spotlight more comfortably, tossed his head back to throw wet hair off his forehead. 'What a miserable night! You should have a rainhat on, Dana. Your hair's going to be soaking wet.

'I'm okay.'

Kurt was holding the light with two hands, keeping it steady on the forward porthole across the bay. Dana worked the toggle switch on top of the light casing— back and forth, back and forth. Remembering her morse code, she changed the rhythm, sending the distinctive SOS in a series of flickers across the bay. It was awkward, standing in the cockpit, leaning over the spotlight. She shifted position, reached out a hand to support herself against Kurt.

'I think we're getting something!' he exclaimed suddenly. 'Take a look!'

Dana switched the beam off and stepped back. A light flickered inside the power boat, then off. Moments later a sound carried across the bay with the wind.

Dana cocked her head, trying to pick the new tone out. 'What's that?'

'His engine. I think he's managed to figure it out. Let's watch for a few minutes and be sure he's okay.'

They huddled together under the shelter of the cockpit dodger, listening to the rain and the wind, watching the boat across the bay as it moved up on its anchor, then steamed across to a safer position on the other shore.

Kurt combed his wet hair back with his fingers. 'I hope he puts out more rode this time.

'Hmm. The wind's letting up now. Hear it?'

'Just for a moment.' He smiled down at her in the half light from the moon. 'How do you feel? You've just completed your first rescue mission.'

'When I first looked, I wasn't really sure if he was over the rock. I didn't know if I should wake you up or not,' she told him.

'If you hadn't, he'd have been on the rocks by morning. Don't ever hesitate to get me up.' She saw a flash of white as he grinned. 'I won't bite you.'

'I wasn't sure. You've been pretty unapproachable the last while.'

'Have I?' He became aware of his arm around her shoulders and dropped it to his side.

As the moon came fully out from behind the clouds, the wind dropped to nothing and silence echoed around them.

Kurt stuffed his hands into his pockets, turning away to look across the bay.

'Don't do that, Kurt,' Dana said softly.

'What?'

'Shut me off, as if I'm not here. You've been doing it ever since . . . I've missed being friends with you.'

The wind played with the damp tendrils of her hair that had escaped from under the hood of her raingear. 'Dana——' He lifted one hand to smooth the damp hairs away from her face. 'I guess I just don't know what to say to you. That night, I—I must have——' He turned away sharply, his hands both back in his pockets. 'I wasn't myself. I'd been dreaming, and when I came up on deck, it was still part of the dream. I had no right to do what I did. I—I damned near raped you, Dana! You must have been terrified.'

He had been too caught up in his memories to realise that she had been more than willing to be in his arms that night. 'Kurt, I didn't——' No. It wouldn't help anything if she told him how she had felt. He plainly didn't want her wanting him. 'I knew you would never hurt me.'

'Thanks for the vote of confidence, but I—thanks.'

The engine from the power boat fell silent. The lights went out, except for the single light at the top of his mast.

'The rain's stopped.' Dana brushed a wet arm across her face.

'Yes. And our mariner in distress is safe and sound. We should go in.'

'Not yet. Let's stay a few minutes more.'

The wind seemed warmer now that the rain had stopped. Kurt undid the buttons on his rain slicker and took it off.

'Kurt?'

'Hmm?'

'Do you—do you think there'll ever be anyone else? After Celeste—three years, that's a long time to be alone.'

'Yes,' he agreed, 'a long time. Let's go in, Dana. It's

past time to go in.'

'And I shouldn't be asking questions—prying.'

'It doesn't matter.' He held the door open for her to go down.

'Doesn't it?' She stopped in the doorway, staring back at him. 'Will you play chess with me again tomorrow night? I've been practising on Andy.'

'I've noticed. Get out of that wet gear before you catch cold. You're shivering.'

'You should change, too. Just because you're bigger, it doesn't mean you can't get sick.'

'All right, we both will. A hot drink would be nice, wouldn't it?'

'Lovely!'

'Get changed, then, and I'll prime the stove.'

Dana half expected that Andy would hear them and get up, demanding to join in their conversation and share their pot of tea. It seemed too good to be true that they were able to settle down together on the settee, sipping from hot mugs, sharing a comfortable silence.

'You're going to sleep.' Kurt leaned over to take her mug. 'Go to bed.'

'No. I'm not tired.'

'Liar. Your eyes were closed. You were starting to snore.'

'I was not!'

'No,' he laughed. 'But you are tired. I've been watching you.' Had he? 'You're working too hard. Don't let Wendy talk you into doing her dishes for her again and you'll have more time for your writing without wearing yourself down.'

'Wendy was tired that day. How did you know about that?'

He laughed. 'I have have my sources—but she wasn't tired. She was lazy, or too doped up with all those pills of hers. Let her do her own work, Dana.'

'What about you? I've seen you—you cooked dinner
for her the other night. And when we stopped at
Ketchikan, look what you let her get away with! It was
her night to cook, so she took us all out to a restaurant—
then you let her sneak out to the ladies' room and leave
you to pay the bill!'

'I'll take it out of Wayne's paycheque,' he promised.

'No, you won't. That's an empty threat. Why do you
let her get away with it?'

'I need Wayne. As long as Wendy's content to be
here, Wayne will keep working. Here, give me your
cup. You really are tired.'

'I haven't finished my tea,' she protested.

'You don't need it.' He put both their cups on the
table, then stood up and drew her to her feet.

'Where are we going next?' Dana asked sleepily.
'When we leave here?'

'Back to Canada. We'll stop in Prince Rupert before
we go to the Queen Charlotte Islands. They'll be having
their sea festival—you'll enjoy that.' Kurt bent down to
press a kiss on her forehead, then gave her a gentle
push. 'Now, go to bed. You're out on your feet.'

When they got to Prince Rupert, Dana went
shopping for a new dress. They were going out to a
nightclub, dancing and dining. 'A little social fling for a
change,' Kurt had suggested.

Wendy perked up. 'Hey, that's a lovely idea! A
civilised evening!'

Dana certainly couldn't go in her blue jeans. She had
to go shopping, but looking through the merchandise in
the dress store, she couldn't help wishing she knew
more about Celeste.

How would Celeste have dressed for an evening out?
Dana wanted to look as different as she could.

Or perhaps she should try to make more of the
fleeting similarity that had entrapped Kurt that night

in Bishop Bay. If she dressed like Celeste——

She shuddered, rejecting the idea. She could only be herself.

The dress was lovely. Surely, when Kurt saw her, he would think she looked nice.

'Very nice,' he said, smiling at her, then at Wendy. 'You're both looking very fetching.'

'Party time,' Wendy declared. 'Enough of sailing and blue jeans.' Kurt nodded, refraining from commenting that he had never seen Wendy in jeans. She went on, 'Tonight is for candlelight and wine, party dresses and romance.' She slipped her hand through Wayne's arm and walked ahead with him to the taxi.

'Coming?' asked Kurt, smiling and offering his arm to Dana. 'You're the lucky lady tonight. You have a dual escort.'

Andy and Kurt. She took both their arms and ran with them to the taxi.

'You're a good sailor now,' Kurt told her her as they followed Wendy into the nightclub. 'We should enter you in the dinghy races—it's the sea festival this weekend—dinghy races, bathtub races—the works!'

'I saw the signs, but you should race the dinghy, Kurt, not me. I'd have fun doing it, but I don't have the skill to win. I don't know what the wind's going to do, how to get the best angle for speed and efficiency. I'd rather watch you race, watch you win.'

She touched his cheek and he looked down at her.

'I'll cheer you on,' she added.

As if he hadn't heard, he pulled the door open and waited for her to precede him. Then they were with the others, being seated at a table overlooking the harbour.

Over dinner they planned the next leg of the cruise, a crossing of the Hecate Strait to the Queen Charlotte Islands.

'My last good sail,' Andy complained. 'So we'd better

have fair winds. Once we get to the Queen Charlottes, I'll have to fly home to get ready for college.'

Wendy groaned, 'There'd better not be winds like we had in Queen Charlotte Sound! I don't need another day like that!'

Dana glanced at Kurt and found him watching her. Did he remember how frightened she had been that day? He smiled slightly and she knew that he did.

'A roaring good sail if we get the winds!' Andy told Wendy, callously cheerful in the face of her protestations of fear. 'Dance, Dana?'

'Not right now. I've got to let my dinner settle. It'll be a good thing when you get back to university, Andy. You'll find some girls there who can keep up with you.'

'But none of them as gorgeous as you, Dana— Wendy, what about you? Will you dance?'

'Only if you call me gorgeous.'

'Gorgeous,' he murmured, a devilish grin on his face.

Wayne smiled at them. 'The next one's mine,' he told Wendy before he turned to speak to Kurt.

'I think I'll enter the dinghy race tomorrow,' Kurt said.

Wayne raised his brows. 'Getting into the local activities? shall we put an autopilot on the dinghy?'

Kurt laughed. 'They'd disqualify me for sure. I don't think electronic aids are allowed.'

'You'll need wind then—and skill. Good luck, Kurt.'

When Andy and Wendy came back to the table, th ey both wished Kurt luck in his race the next day. His eyes met hers across the table.

'Dance, Dana?'

It was a slow love song, perfect for their dance. She turned into his arms as if she belonged there, flowing against him. His arm was at her back. She let her body relax. He couldn't fail to know he had a live woman in his arms. She wasn't going to let him forget that.

His words were low, near her ear. 'You got me into this, but I'm darned if I know why I'm doing it.'

She laughed a soft, husky breath against his shoulder. 'I don't see you being manipulated any further than you want to be.'

His thick eyebrows lifted in a query.

'You'll enjoy it,' she said.

The music stopped. They stood together, between the other couples. Dana didn't move away from Kurt, willing him to keep her in his arms for one more dance.

They danced silently. Dana let the music seep into her along with the feel of Kurt close to her. His hand rested on her back. As they moved, his fingers slid on the soft fabric of her dress, sending pleasurable tremors along her skin.

'Tell me about your family,' she asked him, enjoying the feeling of his arms, hoping he would dance through yet another pause in the music. 'Where did you grow up?'

They turned, Kurt guiding her around a couple who were dancing a fancy, intricate pattern on the wooden floor.

'In California. I had a very dull childhood. I think yours was probably much nicer—I liked your father. Did his family settle on the island?' His hand moved imperceptibly and she was dancing closer, their thighs touching as they moved.

'Dad looks the part of one of the Finnish settlers, doesn't he? Actually, he's a Dane. He was an orphan, adopted by a Finnish couple in Sointula when he was small.'

Kurt eyed her own tall, blonde form in its clinging dress. 'So you're a Danish girl. You and he are cut from the same mould, but your mother is surely not a Dane— or a Finn.'

'Mom's family are Scots. Dad met her on the

mainland and brought her to the island as a bride—she was young, only seventeen.'

Her father had been young, too, when he married, but Dana had always been aware of the strong bond of love between them.

'What happened to his leg?'

'He was bringing his fishing boat in to berth against a log boom. It was slippery, raining. His reverse gear failed and he slipped, fell off the boat into the water between the boat and the log. It—he was in hospital for a long time.'

'It must have been a hard time for all of you.'

'There was a time when we thought he'd never walk again.' If he had died it would have destroyed her mother, and as for Dana, her father had been the rock in her life, the strong, gentle man who had always been there when she needed him.

Kurt didn't dance with her again that night. He talked, mostly with Wayne. Dana joined in the technical conversation where she could, watching Kurt. Why was he avoiding her eyes now—after being so warm to her during their dance?

The next morning dawned bright and hot. Residents said that the sun hardly ever shone in Prince Rupert, but for the Seafest this year it shone with a penetrating heat that could easily have beaten down on a California beach.

Dana dressed in jeans and a light, wispy blouse that let the air through without being revealing. Looking in her mirror she thought she looked ordinary. She couldn't see herself when she moved, the thin, soft fabric moulding to her curves.

Kurt seemed to have caught some of the festival excitement. He was whistling as he cleaned and waxed the bottom of the dinghy.

'You look like a winner this morning!' she told him.

'Where are the others?'

'Andy's found a girl—a redhead from that red sailboat.' He grinned up at her, pausing in his polishing of the dinghy. 'You may have lost yourself a suitor.'

'I'm heartbroken. Can I help with the waxing?'

He considered the shiny white dinghy.

'I think I've pretty well got it. It's time to put it in the water and sail over to the starting line.'

'Where did Wendy and Wayne get to? They were here a few minutes ago when I went to change.'

'They've gone to look for a phone. Wendy wanted to call her mother and talk to the twins; she doesn't like using the radiotelephone. They'll go on to the the festival on their own.'

'Can I sail over with you?' Dana asked.

'Of course.'

The wind was light. They sat in companionable silence, enjoying the motion, basking in the sun as the boat drifted along.

'What will you do after this trip, Kurt?' she enquired.

'I'll have to go back to Montreal and work on setting up production—advertising campaigns to be organised, lining up dealers, working on the export market—and patents, of course, though Andy'll look after that part for me.'

'Andy?'

'Young Andy's father. He looks after the legal details.'

'What about your yacht?'

'I'll leave her in Vancouver. I'll be back this winter for the floating boat show. I've had an exhibit for five years now. Last year, when I was sailing, Roxanne and Andy looked after it for me.'

'Roxanne?' she queried.

'My mother-in-law,' he explained.

'You're very close to your in-laws?'

'They're the only family I have.' Kurt was adjusting the lines, looking at the set of the little sail critically. 'Once the boat show's over, I think I'll go sailing for a year. I'll be ready for the South Seas after all the corporate wheeling and dealing.'

'Will you go alone?'

'Andy'll join me during his holidays.'

She wished she could go with him, to Montreal, to the South Seas—anywhere he wanted to go.

Kurt docked the dinghy at a wharf milling with locals and tourists, holding the boat while Dana got out.

She leaned over, kissing him quickly, feling the cool smoothness of his freshly shaven cheek. 'Good luck. I'll be cheering for you,' she told him.

She watched from the rocks, sitting beside a young boy who borrowed her binoculars and explained,

'My mom's on that boat with the flags on the back. She's a judge for the dinghy race. Really, she's my step-mom. She's tops! My dad's over at the loudspeaker—he'll be giving out some of the prizes. I'm David. What's your name?'

He was good company. They watched together as Kurt won, agreeing that he sailed better than any of the opponents.

''Bye, David! I'm going to meet Kurt!' Dana had to shout over the noise of a formation of seaplanes flying overhead in a display of the town's air power.

The crowd was thick, milling about in anticipation of the start of the bathtub races. Dana pushed through, finally arriving at the dock just as Kurt landed the dinghy.

'Congratulations! I was cheering for you.'

'That must have been what did it.' He smiled at her and her breath caught in her throat. 'I caught that wind just at the right time. If I hadn't tacked just then, that red catboat would have beat me.'

She linked her arm with his. 'We'll lose each other in this crowd.'

'Hang on, then. One of the judges told me the presentation would be after the bathtub race. Why don't we find a spot to watch while we wait?'

Kurt looked oddly embarrassed as he accepted the trophy. Dana caught his hand afterwards and they pushed their way through the crowd, holding hands.

'I've heard there's going to be street dancing tonight,' she said. 'Apparently, in the past years they didn't have street dancing, but today——'

'Where'd you get your information? Your friend David?'

'He was very helpful. Shall we try to find the dancing?' she suggested.

'I'd rather find something to eat. Let's take the dinghy back and go round up dinner.'

They found a water-front restaurant, crowded to overflowing. Kurt didn't seem to mind waiting for a seat, so they stood at the entrance amid a small crowd, smiling at each other over the pompous man who was showing off for his guests as he placed an unnecessarily complex order.

Later, they went walking along the water-front, watching the last of the Seafest activity on the water, talking lazily, enjoying the sun and the quiet of the shore as they moved away from the crowd. They were looking for Wendy and Wayne as they walked, but Kurt didn't expect to find them.

'They'll be inside where Wendy can have a drink,' he predicted, 'but I don't want to go pub crawling looking for them. They'll find their way home. Let's stay out here.'

They walked, stepping out of the way of children on bicycles, even becoming involved in a teenage soccer game in a small neighbourhood park.

'I don't think that's my game,' Dana told him,
breathless, as they walked away from the little park. 'I
didn't do well.'

'With all the talents you have, I wouldn't worry about
the soccer!'

It was very late when they moved together through
the silent mystery of the boats on the darkened wharf.
Silence, except for the creaking of fenders against the
vessels, the occasional murmur of a hidden voice.

They stepped aboard the darkened yacht, feeling
their way through the cockpit, down the companionway. No lights on. Everyone else was either asleep or
still out on the town.

'Don't turn on the electrics!' Dana begged Kurt as he
reached for a switch. 'Light a lantern.'

His lighter flicked. The cabin was bathed in orange
light from the kerosene lantern.

'Kurt?' In the half light she drew a shaky breath and
reached up to touch his face. 'Kurt, how can you be so
warm to me as a friend, yet so unwilling to love?
How——?'

He took her fingers, grasped them with his and drew
them away. Her fingers were trembling, or his
fingers—she wasn't sure which.

'Dana, don't say any more. You'll wish you hadn't,
come morning.'

'It's been three years, Kurt—three years! Surely, in
all that time——'

'You think three years is long enough? Three years is
no time at all.'

'That night in Bishop Bay——'

'It wasn't you in my arms that night.'

'It *was* me. You know it was me. I'm here, Kurt, and
I'm real.' She reached her lips to brush his mouth in a
soft declaration of her love.

Did she imagine a faint twinge of response? She

moved closer. For a moment, when his hands took life, pulling her closer, she thought she was imagining it— wanting it so badly she'd dreamed it.

He brushed his mouth against hers and she opened her lips, sliding her arms up around his neck, letting her fingers spread through his soft hair, responding passionately as he took charge of the kiss.

He moved to the settee, taking her with him. Her legs were weak, no longer able to hold her. She wanted to lean back, enjoy his hands on her, his lips on her skin. His mouth left hers and travelled down, stirring to life every inch of skin along her throat.

'Please love me,' she whispered against his hair.

A shudder went through him as he moved away from her. A light flashed outside as a boat steamed past in the dark, and Kurt stood up abruptly, putting the width of the cabin between them.

'Kurt?'

'Dana, you can't be second-best, a substitute for another woman!' He knew as he spoke that it wasn't entirely true. Dana, with her generous curves and her passionate nature, stirred a response in him that he had never felt with Celeste.

Love.

He felt guilt rising up, as if Celeste were warm and living, waiting in his home, and he was here with this woman in his arms.

Dana shivered in the coolness of the night.

'I care about you, Danish girl. But I can't——'

'You can't go on for ever loving a dead woman. Three years, Kurt—three years come and gone. You've changed in those years. You're not the same man who loved Celeste. You've changed, and she hasn't been here to keep up.'

'Dana, don't——'

'You're running away from life, living in the past. It's

easy to love a dead woman, isn't it? It may be lonely, but a dead woman can't ask anything of you. Is that safer? She can't leave you, can't fail you. Is that why, Kurt? If so, you're wrong. She can't fail you bacause she isn't there.'

His face was frozen, cold and hard, so that she trembled as he made an angry motion towards her, but she couldn't stop the flow of words coming from her.

'You can't touch her, Kurt! If you talk to her, you're only talking to yourself. Kurt, you can't make love to her—not ever again!'

She slipped away, leaving him with empty arms, the echo of her voice intruding on his memories.

CHAPTER FIVE

ONCE they were underway again, Dana spent time
giving the galley a real clean-up. In the afternoon she
took all the brass lanterns on deck and sat in the cockpit
polishing them. Kurt was there steering.

He ignored her at first. She worked quietly, polishing
brass, but with the sun overhead and her own naturally
vibrant spirits, she soon started talking, chattering—
and finally he smiled a little at her. She knew that he
was still angry with her, but he hadn't the temperament
to stay angry, and the tension between them gradually
relaxed.

The hot, clear weather held, but the air was still.
There was no point putting sails up. They glided along
under engine power, passing islands and lighthouses as
they moved west.

In the early evening Kurt put up the stays'l and
mizzen just before Dana's watch began. Soon they
would be in the open, crossing the Hecate Strait
overnight so that they could arrive at the Queen
Charlotte Islands during daylight the next day.

'My watch now,' she told him, moving in front of
him to the wheel. 'We could use more sail, couldn't we?'

Dana wanted speed this evening. She would have
welcomed the tearing pace of a wild sail on a gale.

'We'll leave it as it is.' Kurt was watching the sky
ahead of them, his normally smooth face roughened
with the faint shadow of a beard. 'We won't know what
it's like in Hecate Strait until we round the tip of this
island.'

'Oh, come on, Kurt! We have only half our sails up!

I'll put them up—you don't have to bother.'

'Restless tonight, aren't you, Danish girl?' He was watching her with an amused tolerance that she found irritating. Celeste would never have argued like this, she realised, meeting his eyes.

'Yes. Yes, I am.'

'Put them up if you want but if they have to come back down, you take them down yourself.'

'I won't have to. Look at the water! It's just a light breeze.'

'I wouldn't place any bets on that.'

He disappeared below. Just as well. Dana was in a strange mood. If he'd stayed she might have said anything; she had already said too much.

With the steering on autopilot, she went forward and raised the jib, then the main. They picked up speed and were going along nicely, skimming the water at the north end of Stephens Island. Perhaps the wind had increased while she was hoisting sails, because they were really moving now, although the waves were still small.

She fiddled with the trim of the sails, letting them out as the wind swung father to the south, getting every knot of speed possible out of the moving air. By the time they came around Stephens Island, the wind had freshened and she had her exciting ride. She had taken the steering off autopilot, enjoying the feel of handling the wheel herself.

She stood in the cockpit with her legs astride, her hair streaming out in the wind. She spun the wheel, anticipating each swing of the bow as the waves surged under them. She was busy with the steering, the wheel wilder every minute.

She laughed. This was the feeling that kept skiers going down the downhill runs, kept racing drivers on the track. When Kurt came out she grinned at him, still laughing.

'Don't you dare tell me you're taking the helm,' she called to him.

He shook his head, leaning back in the far corner of the cockpit as if he meant to stay a while.

'Enjoying yourself?' he asked.

'I am!'

The waves were getting bigger. It occurred to her that the ride could be rough for the people down below.

'Where's Wendy?' asked Dana.

'Taken to her bed. I sent Andy to bed, too. He's got to get up to be on watch later tonight.'

'And Wayne?' She spun the wheel quickly to catch the surge of a monstrous wave. She had to swing it back at once to stop the ship swinging around to broach as they went down in the trough between waves.

'Wayne's reading a book on designing micro-processor circuits. Don't worry, Danish girl—nothing you do to this yacht is going to get through his concentration.'

'We're doing over nine knots,' she told him. When she looked at him, she found him watching her with wry amusement, as if she were a strange creature he hadn't yet discovered how to handle.

'Just what do you think I'm going to do?' she laughed.

'Well, you're not going to sink us. I'll make sure of that!'

'That's a nasty crack!' she accused him, then she couldn't talk because the waves were getting bigger. She had to concentrate everything on the steering. She reached over to switch on the autopilot, to relieve her tiring arms of the task of steering.

'I wouldn't,' Kurt told her. He'd moved closer to her so that he didn't have to shout. 'The autopilot won't be able to stabilize the course in these waves—you'll swing all over the place if you try to turn it on now.'

If anyone knew what the autopilot was capable of, he did. Dana concentrated on steering. It had ben fun, a wild ride, but steering in this sudden storm, she was courting the edge of disaster. They had too much sail up for the wind. *Windflower II* was wheeling out of control. Dana was fighting the wheel to keep on course.

If she hadn't been the one to insist on putting the sails up, she'd be turning to Kurt, asking him to take over, get her out of this mess. Kurt was standing at her side, ready to bail her out if she couldn't handle the situation she'd created.

She was damned if she would show defeat that easily.

Wind on the coast was almost always gusty. If she could hang on, sooner of later it would blow itself out and she'd be able to get the autopilot back on. Once she had the ship under electronic control, she could start getting sails down. Kurt, beside her, would help if she asked.

She wasn't going to ask.

She thought her arms would drop from the wheel, or freeze with fatigue, trying to keep everything going more or less in a westerly direction. The wind was behind them. They were running hard, the large mass of sail catching in the gusts, throwing the small ship off course as she dropped from the crest of the waves.

Dana reached the point when she couldn't tell where they were. She had only the compass to guide her in a wild ride. After a time she found that it was easier, the steering had settled and she had longer between spins of the wheel.

Miraculously, the wind had lightened. Dana waited for a moment when they were riding straight and level on top of a large wave, then quickly switched the autopilot on. In front of her, the dial swung sharply, hunting, then settled as the computer found their course.

'Good work, Dana!' His hands were on her shoulders, drawing her away from the wheel. Her own hands, gripping the now useless steering wheel, dropped to her sides. 'You did a hell of a job of handling that!'

'If they had a ride like that at the Pacific National Exhibition, they'd make a million on it!' Despite her exhaustion, she still felt the excitement of those wild seas. She had been frightened, terrified she'd lose control and the vessel would broach.

'We'd better get those sails down before the wind comes up again. I'll get the harness.'

'I'll do it, Kurt. I said I'd do it.'

He ignored her, disappearing below.

She had been the one to raise the damned sails; she'd get them down on her own!

She moved out of the security of the empty cockpit, holding on to the handrails. The deck was heaving beneath her feet and she stumbled, weaving against the motion of the ocean.

The wind was already coming up again, filling the sails hard and bringing the wildness back. Hoping the autopilot would keep up with the twisting of the waves, Dana grasped the mast, holding on as the deck below her tilted sharply away. From the cockpit it had seemed safe enough, but out on this wide expanse of heaving deck she felt terribly vulnerable to the angry ocean.

If she could get that big jib down, the boat might stabilise. She had the sheet in her hands when Kurt's arms came around both her and the mast, crushing her against the mast and tearing the rope out of her hands.

'Get this harness on! Then go back to the cockpit!'

His eyes were blazing. He had snapped the line from his harness on to a nearby shackle and he was pulling

the second harness over her shoulders, snapping her
line beside his.

'What the hell do you think you're doing, going out
on deck without a harness in these conditions?'

She could feel the roughness of his unshaven cheek
against her hair. She pulled back, using the little room
between him and the mast.

'You said I was to take them down and I will! Go
back!' He'd never hear her if her voice wasn't raised to
a shout. 'I'll take them down myself!'

She pushed away his hand, breaking free of his arms
and catching hold of the jib halyard.

'Don't be a damned fool! There's too much wind!'

She kept moving, holding the halyard in one hand
and making for the foredeck.

'Dana, so help me, if you go out on the bowsprit——'
He grabbed her roughly, pulling her back so that they
fell together against the mast. He secured them both
with one long, strong arm. 'Dammit, Dana!' He glared
down at her, silencing her with a deep blue look from
his eyes.

The storm was howling around them. It was crazy to
think she could hear her own heart against all that
wind. Yet it pounded wildly in her ears as his eyes froze
on her face, as he moved slowly closer.

The unshaven skin of his face bit into her skin as
their lips met, as he drew her hard against him with his
one free arm. With the howling of the wind, the
crashing of the wild Pacific, Dana found herself
clinging to Kurt, both arms around his neck, their lips
fused in a deep, intimate kiss. She was shaking when he
drew his head back. He wasn't any steadier. His voice
was low and unsteady.

'What a hell of a time you're picking for an
argument! My God, you're a stubborn woman!' He
thrust the jib halyard back into her hands. 'Stay here.

When I get out on the bowsprit, let the sail down slowly and I'll gather it in. And for God's sake, hang on! That harness will keep you with the boat, but it won't stop you from falling.'

Then he was working his way around the flying sail, out to the end of the bowsprit where she couldn't help feeling that the stainless steel rails of the pulpit weren't enough to keep him safe in this heaving sea.

She let the sail down slowly, watching him gather it in, careful not to let it get away from her so that Kurt could control the folds of the fabric as he stuffed them into the sail bag.

Then Kurt was back, tying off the halyard and stopping her hands as they reached for the mainsail halyard.

'We'll never get the main down in this wind. Go to the cockpit and take the steering off autopilot. Point her up into the wind and I'll get the main down.' He stared down at her when she hesitated. 'And for heaven's sake, don't argue! If you want to fight, we'll fight later—when it's calm.'

'You need a shave,' she retorted, grinning at him, moving away from him, taking her safety line and moving it from place to place as she worked her way carefully back to the cockpit.

With the sail shortened, they resumed their westward journey, steady and stable in the wind, ploughing through the waves towards the setting sun.

Together, they watched in silence as the red gathered in the sky and the flaming sun sank into the water. Darkness surrounded them with shadows.

'You'd better go down for some sleep,' his quiet voice reached her on the wind.

'You're always telling me to go to sleep. I'm not tired.' She was zinging with energy, the adrenalin licking along her veins. 'Can't I stay up here for a while?'

The faint red light from the compass showed her his smile.

'Are you willing to fight for the privilege?'

She had been ready to fight for the right to hoist the sails; the right to take them back down. Then, when he kissed her on the deck, she had abruptly lost her desire to fight.

'I think I've had enough fighting. I just want to stay out here.'

'For a little while. Then you have to sleep.'

Out on the deck in the midst of the storm, he had pulled her roughly into his arms and kissed her as if she belonged to him, as if she were all he'd ever wanted in life.

She stood in the cockpit beside him, hugging that knowledge to herself.

At first she sat very silently, sharing the dark without talking, watching the water ahead for a shadow that might mean a log floating in their path. From time to time, Kurt went through the doors into the aft cabin, noting their speed and heading on the chart, calculating their landfall on the other side of the strait.

As the night settled more heavily on them, the wind dropped slightly, leaving them sailing smoothly on a beam reach.

'Are you going to put up more sail?' she asked him at last, her voice crossing the darkness between them.

'Are you insisting?' His voice held laughter.

'No! I'm not about to argue with you over the sails again—at least, not until I have a lot more experience.'

He laughed aloud. 'You're prickly today, Danish girl, I haven't seen that side of you before. You're right about the sails, though. Normally, I'd put the jib back up in this wind, but if I do we'll go too fast. I don't want to get to the other side of this channel until it's daylight again.'

That made sense. Even with radar, there was no point trying to make a landfall in the darkness.

'When I was in my teens,' Dana told him some time in the darkest hour, 'I used to dream I was fishing with my dad. I went a couple of times, and I loved the night fishing—gliding along the water, Dad and I alone on the deck. It's such a secret time. I used to dream he'd take me and we'd head west in the night—and just keep going.'

In the darkness she could hardly see him when the only cloud in the sky drifted across the moon.

'Have you ever crossed an ocean, Kurt?'

'Yes.'

'Where?'

'From San Francisco to Hawaii, then across to Australia.'

'And back? Which way back?'

'New Zealand ... the Society Islands ... the Galapagos—I came back the slow way, island-hopping, stopping whenever I found a place to interest me.' He laughed softly at himself. 'They all interested me. I never did get back to San Francisco. I went through Panama, visited the West Indies.'

The West Indies wasn't far from Bermuda, the memory that had brought shadows to Kurt's face. Bermuda had something to do with Celeste. Dana wasn't about to ask, to bring the shadows back to life between them.

'Tell me about the West Indies,' she invited.

He told her and she listened, fascinated, seeing every village he visited, every friend he made.

Of course there had been women too. He had been single then, before he met Celeste. He mentioned a family in Grenada and their daughter Janice. Listen-

ing, Dana felt an inexplicable certainty that Janice and
Kurt had been lovers.

'Did you visit Janice when you brought *Windflower
II* around to the west coast?' she asked.

'Yes.' He laughed. 'They met me at the wharf—
Janice and her husband and their four sons, They took
me home to dinner—a real family feast it was, too. I
don't know when I'd enjoyed a meal so much——'

She could see him at a large family gathering, sitting
back, enjoying the banter around him, listening.

He was a family man without a family.

'The article Dad read——'

'That was written when I was in the West Indies the
first time.'

'How did you get the boat?'

'She belonged to my father. He left her to me when he
died.'

The moon had emerged from its shroud. Kurt's face
was illuminated, the high cheekbones throwing a deep
shadow across his eyes.

'How old were you?' asked Dana.

'Eighteen. I was at university. I finished my degree,
then went sailing.'

'You mother? What about your mother?'

'I can't remember her. She died when I was very
small—your time's up, Dana. Don't forget, you'll have
to get up in the morning to relieve Andy on the wheel.'

'Good night, then.' She took his cup and her own and
left him alone in the darkness of the cockpit.

Kurt had been alone all his life, except for the few
years with Celeste—certainly, there had always been
friends, but no one to call his own. There might have
been his father, but she had heard a remoteness in
Kurt's voice when he mentioned his parents. Celeste
had been his only family. He had reached out to her,

and lost her. Could she blame him for not wanting to risk again?

She slept at last, tossing restlessly as they crossed the strait in the darkness, waking to a brilliant dawn.

Just after sunrise, she found Wendy in the galley, rubbing her forehead, staring at the coffee pot as if she could will it to boil.

'Morning, Wendy. How are you this morning?'

'This open water is the pits. I've had enough of it. Come to that, I've had enough of this sailing nonsense.'

'We're almost at the other side. It's certainly not rough now.'

'I suppose not,' Wendy admitted grudgingly as she took the coffee percolator off the flame, 'but we have to go back across this bloody stretch of water, you know. Last night was—I've been talking to Wayne. He says they're done testing. We could leave. There's an airport on the Charlottes, daily jet service to Vancouver. We could fly home. Wayne could start working on things in Montreal—all that bits and bytes stuff he has to do before they can actually start production.'

Dana slid a cup out of the holder on the wall, held it out for Wendy to fill.

'I like sailing when it's calm. Not this nonsense driving through the night into storms. What if we hit something? What if we lost our way?'

Last night had been exciting for Dana, tearing along the water, crossing the strait. Dana thought she could enjoy crossing an ocean, but it had been different for Wendy. Wendy had been below, in her bunk, terrified.

Andy was at the wheel. Actually, the wheel was inactive and Andy was reading a book, glancing up occasionally to watch for floating logs and check the trim of the sails.

'Morning, beautiful!' he greeted Dana as she joined him. 'You see what's ahead? Land. Any sign of breakfast down there?'

'Wendy's cook and she's just getting organised. I brought you a coffee.'

'Lovely! Give it here.'

'When do you fly home, Andy?'

'Day after tomorrow. Kurt called through and made the reservation from Prince Rupert.'

'Getting eager to get back to it?'

'Not yet. I wish I could stay at least another month and cruise down the east coast of the Charlottes.'

These islands might have been the land that time forgot. Islanders referred to Island Time as if it ran differently from mainland time. Everyone seemed relaxed, in no hurry.

Except Kurt.

Once they crossed the Hecate Strait, it seemed to Kurt that he was losing control of everything—the voyage, his own emotions, his life.

The Hectic Strait, Dana had called it after her wild ride with too much sail up.

Andy was packing, getting ready to go home. He would be missed. Without him, the work of sailing would descend totally on Kurt and Dana.

As a passenger, Wendy was beginning to get on Kurt's nerves with her helpless determination to be virtually useless, but he didn't want her to leave, taking Wayne and leaving him alone with Dana.

Damn her ridiculous fears! She'd egged Wayne on until he finally took Kurt aside on the wharf at Queen Charlotte.

The testing was done. Wayne's function on board was complete. Whatever was left to do could more easily be done back in Montreal. And Wendy was so unhappy, missing her children, terrified of crossing the Hecate Strait again.

What could he say? He could hardly tell Wayne that

he was terrified, of being alone with a perfectly charming young woman!

Dana.

He'd been so long without a woman. Was that why he had started dreaming of Dana these last few nights? She was young and beautiful and available. Of course he wanted her. As a one-night stand he could handle it, but she was a warm woman with her own needs.

After Celeste's death, he had done his time in that introspective hell his life had become. The needing and the wanting. The love turned to pain.

It had taken a long time—too long—but he'd finally regained control, started to reform his life. He had to keep control. Couldn't allow anyone to put him so much at risk again.

He found Dana in the galley.

'Cooking? Isn't it Wendy's day?'

'Wendy's packing. She says she's taking us all out to dinner. I think she's forgotten about lunch.'

'If she's taking us to dinner,' he said wryly, 'I'd better be sure I've got money with me.'

Dana shook her head. He watched the soft, fair hair settle around her shoulders, remembering how silky it had felt in his fingers.

'Kurt, surely she wouldn't do that again? Leave you to pay the bill——'

'I wouldn't want you to be disillusioned. I'll treat us to dinner— there's a hotel with a dance floor, I hear. How about dinner and dancing?'

'Sounds lovely.'

Why had he made that offer? He wanted her in his arms again, but without the risk. Dancing was safer, had an ending where he dropped his arms and turned away.

'Perhaps you should think about flying home, Dana. With Wayne and Wendy going——'

The articles aren't finished. The magazine wants two more articles. They particularly want the one on the Queen Charlottes.'

'I'll send you pictures. I'll send you a copy of the ship's log.'

'It's not the same. You know it's not the same. I can't write an article about a place I've never been. I've got to see it, know what it's like.'

The silence was uncomfortable. He found his own hands shaking, his voice unsteady.

'I don't think this is a good idea, Danish girl. You and I, alone on this ship.'

'You could send for friends to join us. You'd better if you're so afraid of being alone with me. Because I'm not leaving, not unless you throw me off. I've got commitments, articles to write.

She banged a plate of sandwiches down on the table, tossed back that silky hair and rang the ship's bell to call the others to lunch.

Kurt couldn't help laughing—but he couldn't imagine throwing her off his ship.

He found himself at the phone booth in the hotel, starting his trans-continental search for Harriet and Brent, chasing his friends halfway across the world with an invitation that had a tinge of desperation in it.

Dana went to town with Wendy, but there were no stores and Wendy quickly lost interest. Dana could have suggested they stop at the hotel to look up Harold. He would have welcomed her visit, and Wendy would have been interested to see an old flame of Dana's. But she couldn't feel any enthusiasm for a meeting with Harold.

For dinner that night Dana wore the dress she'd bought in Prince Rupert. Kurt had done a good job of ignoring her all day, ever since that morning when he'd suggested she leave the ship. So far as she could tell, he

wasn't even aware that she was looking nice this
evening. When they settled at the table in the dining
room, he was deep in conversation with Wayne. Wayne
was listening, nodding, and neither of them knew or
cared about the two women across from them.

Dana was listening, too. Kurt was talking future
plans. and that had a place in her articles. She asked
some questions, made notes of details that could fit into
the final article.

'By the time it's on the market,' she told Kurt, 'you'll
have them lined up to buy that system for their boats.'

'You may be right,' he agreed, his attention finally
turning to her. 'The last letter I got from Andy and
Roxanne said they'd already had a couple of enquiries.'

'That's a bit too early, isn't it? The first article
doesn't go to press until next month.'

'True. But apparently this month's issue bills your
series as a coming event—complete with mention of
past successes of my propeller and a hint of a new
system to be unveiled in your articles.'

That was wonderful news. He might have told her
before, but she shrugged that away. If the articles
meant sales for his system, surely he wouldn't send her
away before the cruise was over.

The waitress came, assuring them that the salmon
was freshly caught by local fishermen. They all ordered
Pacific salmon. A small local band strummed background music as they ate, then burst into full song as a
pretty vocalist joined them. She sang a haunting song
about her love. Wendy led Wayne out on to the floor.
Dana looked at Kurt, but he wasn't going to dance. He
had his wallet out and was withdrawing a telephone
company credit card.

'I'll see you later,' he told Andy, his eyes avoiding
Dana. 'I'm going to use the hotel phone. I'm trying to
get hold of Brent—he and Harriet might like to fly out

and join us for the trip south. Apparently they're at the house in Bermuda.'

'That's a good idea,' Andy agreed. 'They'll probably leap at the chance. Come on, Dana, let's dance.'

Moving on the dance floor with Andy, Dana could see Kurt as he walked through the doorway towards the lobby.

'Who are Harriet and Brent?' she asked.

'Harriet's my cousin—Brent's her boy-friend. They live together.'

'Would they be free to come on such short notice?'

'Brent's a writer, I guess he can work anywhere he wants to. Right now I think they're at the cottage in Bermuda—it's Dad's cottage, but everyone in the family uses it. You've heard of Austin Trent? That's Brent.'

'Of course I've heard of Trent.' *Murder in Bermuda, Murder in a Small Closet*—who hadn't heard of Trent's prolific output of tantalising puzzlers? Any other time she would be eager to meet the man—but not now. Not if he and his Harriet came out here as a buffer between Kurt and Dana.

The music turned wild and Dana moved away from Andy, dancing a pattern around him, laughing because this youngster could hardly keep up with her pace. Laughter kept the tears back. After two fast numbers, the vocalist took the microphone again and began another haunting tale.

'Thank goodness!' gasped Andy, moving into the steps of a waltz. 'I couldn't have taken another.'

'You're out of shape,' she taunted him.

'I think I'm about to get my rest. There's a fellow coming our way. Unless I miss my guess, he plans to cut in on me. I think he knows you—looks like he can't believe his eyes, seeing you here. Thirtyish, about my height, dark hair.'

'That'll be Harold.'

'Harold?' he querried.

'A friend of mine. He lives up here, manages the hotel.'

And of course it was Harold who tapped Andy on the shoulder. 'May I? Dana, I couldn't believe it when you turned up here! Where'd you spring from?'

Andy let her go unwillingly. He hadn't had Dana in his arms very often; he'd been enjoying it immensely, though knowing it wouldn't last.

'I sailed in,' Dana told Harold, letting him lead her away, following his steps with no effort. He was a good dancer; they had danced many a night away in Vancouver.

'The big ketch that came in yesterday? Don't look so surprised. Everyone in town knows when a new boat comes in. It's a small town. But how did you come to be on that boat?'

'I'm writing a series on the cruise and some equipment that's being tested out on board.'

'What about your job?'

'I've quit.'

'Pretty rash, my dear.' They turned to avoid another couple. Dana knew the instant Kurt entered the room again. He sat down at the table across from Andy. She watched them talking, willed Kurt to look up and see her. He laughed at something Wendy said, but he didn't look up. It didn't matter to him at all that she was in the arms of a strange man.

'I'll find another job,' she told Harold.

'That's easier said than done, You should have——'

'Don't, Harold. Don't lecture me.'

He frowned, She had always fascinated him, partly because he could never get close to her. Whenever he reached out to Dana, it seemed she slipped away from him.'

'I could find you something here,' he told her now. 'In the hotel, or elsewhere in the town.'

'Thanks, Harold, but I don't think so. I want to finish this cruise.'

'Afterwards——?'

'No.' It had been no when Harold left Vancouver, when he had asked her to come with him. It was still no.

'All right, but what about tonight? How long are you staying?'

'I don't know. Tomorrow some of the guests are taking the jet to Vancouver. We'll be seeing them off.'

'Tonight you're free?'

'I guess I am.'

'Then give me tonight, for old times' sake.'

She shook her head, watching the table, watching Wendy and Wayne and Andy. Kurt raised his head, met her eyes for a cold moment, then turned back to the others.

'Come on, Dana, we'll drive out to the beach. You always loved walking on the beach at night. Remember the night we danced at the Devonshire, then drove to Kits beach and walked on the sand until dawn?'

'I remember.' He had kissed her on the beach and his arms had been pleasant around her. Not like Kurt's arms. Kurt's arms coaxed the wild yearning from her, but Kurt was going to hold his sad memories close for ever.

'All right,' she agreed. 'I'll come. A walk on the beach would be nice.'

They finished the dance first, then walked towards the table where the others talked.

'This is Harold,' Dana announced to the four at the table. They all knew; Andy had told them. She introduced him to each one of them anyway. When she said Kurt's name, he nodded to Harold. Harold put his hand on her shoulder at that moment, as if in a gesture

of possession. He must have sensed something, though
Kurt obviously couldn't care less what man she was
with.   ·

'Have a seat,' Wendy urged Harold. 'Join us.'

'I'd like to,' he smiled at Wendy with just the right
degree of regret, 'but Dana and I were going to drive up
the coast. We should leave before it gets dark.'

Nobody was going to stop them. Kurt didn't care.
Somehow she had thought it might get through to him,
her going off with another man, but he was already
turning away.

Harold stopped to tell the waiter that dinner was on
the house for Kurt's party, then he took Dana north on
the highway.

He pulled off the road into a private driveway. 'We
can get to the beach from here.'

'The owners of the house——'

'It's my house.'

He led her down a well-worn path to the beach. She
walked towards the water, slipping her shoes off.

'We should have brought a drink.' She wasn't much
of a drinker, but tonight she felt she could use
something.

'Wait right there just a moment.'

While he was gone, Dana slipped off her nylons and
put them into her bag, wanting the feel of the sand on
her feet.

He was back in a moment, two glasses of wine in his
hands. She took her glass from him and sipped a little,
then drank it down.

'First time I've seen you belt it back like that. Do you
want another?'

'No.' She felt vaguely nauseated.

He linked his hand with hers and they walked along
the beach. She asked him about his house, about the
islands. She listened while he talked, making no protest

when his arm slipped around her shoulders, when he bent and kissed her lips lightly.

She let him lead her back to the house, accepted another glass of wine. Standing by the window, looking out over the beach in the half light of dusk, she drank the wine while Harold lit a fire in his fireplace.

Then he came over to her and drew her into his arms. He looked down at her strangely before he kissed her, then his arms pulled her close and she felt his hands on her back, sliding over her.

Dana felt it all, and if her body made some small response to him, it was nothing in her heart. Instead, she found tears slipping down her cheeks.

She didn't want this. Harold was her friend, but she couldn't take comfort from him this way. When he touched her, she found herself yearning for Kurt. If she let passion overtake her in Harold's arms, it would be a pretence she'd hate herself for in the morning.

'What the hell?' His hands had moved to her face, caressing her cheek, and he had found the wet trail of her tears. She pulled away, turning back to the window, rubbing her eyes with the back of her hands.

'I'm sorry,' she muttered.

'It's the tall fellow—Kurt. You're mixed up with him.'

'No—yes. Yes, I'm sorry.'

'Then why did he let you come with me? You had a fight?'

'He doesn't want me.'

'And you thought I might make a good substitute? Or was I supposed to make him jealous? Is he going to come bursting in here?'

'No. No, he won't. I'm sorry for this, but—will you please take me back?'

'Back to the boat? To him?'

'Yes.'

He shook his head angrily, 'I'm damned if I will, Dana! You can't just—oh, hell! I'll take you back. Of course I'll take you back. But we'll have a coffee first. Go and wash and I'll make the coffee.'

She let him guide her to the bathroom and she stood in front of his mirror, staring at her grubby face. The tears had made her mascara run, then she'd smudged it into a mess by wiping her eyes with her hands, She washed it all off, leaving her face pale and colourless.

Harold served her coffee, telling her how he'd found this house, what he planned to do with it. She hardly heard a word he said, but she was thankful that he kept up the pretence, talking about things that didn't require more than a nod from her throughout the drive back to the government wharfs.

He stopped her a few feet before they reached the yacht, holding her with hands gentle on her shoulders.

'You don't need to go back, Dana. You could stay,' he told her softly.

'No.'

'No conditions, You can have a room at the hotel. You'd find a job easily enough, and another place to stay if you wanted. If——'

'Thank you, Harold, but no.' He wasn't much taller than her. It was easy to reach up and place a light kiss on his lips. 'You're a dear man, and I wish I could be in love with you. Goodbye, Harold.'

She slipped away quickly, before he could say anything more.

She saw the shadow in the cockpit. She knew it was Kurt, knew long before she reached him.

She could feel his anger before she heard the tightness of his voice.

'Where the hell have you been? Do you know what time it is?'

'What time is it?' Dana felt dizzy. The coffee hadn't

completely cancelled the effect of wine.

'Three o'clock. Three o'clock in the morning.' She shivered at the cold in his voice.

'You didn't have to wait up for me.'

He could see her face in the light from the cockpit. The make-up she had worn earlier was gone, her face swollen slighlty. Swollen from passion. Kurt's imagination readily supplied a picture of Dana in Harold's arms, her creamy skin flushed from his touch.

He had been seeing them together ever since Dana had walked out of the hotel dining room, and now—with the evidence of her newly scrubbed, flushed face in front of him—the furious anger he had held at bay welled up uncontrollably in him.

'It didn't take long, did it?' he taunted her angrily, hardly knowing where the words came from. 'The first good-looking man to come near you, and you're gone, jumping into his bed.'

'You're jumping to conclusions, aren't you? Or do you subscribe to the view that a couple out after eleven must be——?'

'You left your stockings in his bedroom,' he told her, looking down at the shoes in her hand, her bare legs below them. He brushed his hand roughly along her cheek, cursing himself for wanting her so much. 'And your make-up's gone. Did he make a mess of it?'

'I've known Harold for years. We're——'

'Go to bed, Dana. I don't want to hear it.'

She started to turn away, then swung back angrily.

'Just where do you get off? Who do you think you are, sitting out here, waiting to lecture me on my morals? I'd take that from my father. I'd take it from a lover. But you're not a lover—remember that, Kurt. You didn't want to be my lover. You're just the man who owns this boat, and I'm your passenger. It isn't your business where I spend my nights. I can sleep in anyone's bed, any night I choose, and it's nothing to you!'

Don't go to him again, he wanted to shout at her. His hands clenched, wanting to take her shoulders and shake her hard. The hurt was boiling up in him fast, threatening the little control he had left. He clenched his jaw hard and turned away, striding across the deck without caring who might be disturbed below.

He escaped into the darkness, pacing the seashore of the little port until coolness returned, until he was master of himself again.

CHAPTER SIX

WHILE Kurt was paying the taxi driver, Dana got out quickly, moving away.

'Where are you going?' he called after her.

'Into town.' Anywhere. Nowhere. Just away for a while. They'd been to the airport, watched the jet fly away with Wendy, Wayne and Andy aboard. Kurt had been silent, almost surly, all morning.

That was fine with her. The last thing she wanted this morning was even a moment's conversation with him.

'Can't you stay away from Harold? Is he that good?'

She turned furiously at his taunt, found him looking strangely tired, the lines of his face deeply etched.

'You——' she began.

'Would you mind waiting, going later?' His tone was carefully neutral. She must have imagined the fury in his voice a moment ago. 'I've got some work to do on the engine. I'll need help.'

Dana shrugged, turned back, walked down the ramp ahead of him.

She passed him a screwdriver when he asked for it.

'Hold this wrench, would you?' he asked, not looking at her.

I'd like to hit you over the head with it, she thought. You won't even look at me, yet last night——

She held the wrench. Silently.

When he was buried in engine parts and seemed to have no need of her, she would have gone out again. She wanted to find a beach and pace it, alone, until her mind straightened out and she could stop feeling hurt

110

and angry and irrational.

Kurt had blocked the passage to the exit with hatchcovers and toolboxes. If she asked him to move everything, make a passage for her to get out, he might—or he might ignore her.

If she really wanted to go, she could exit by an undignified wriggle out the skylight in the forward cabin.

According to the schedule, Kurt was cook today. She doubted if the schedule meant much when three of the five people on it were a hundred miles away by this time. She thought of an omelette, but with Kurt buried in the engine it might be an hour before he emerged to eat. Heaven knew why she was thinking of feeding him when he was being so miserable. She should walk out, never come back.

She opened a tin of salmon and made sandwiches, sliced and wrapped them and put them in the fridge. She tossed a salad to go with the sandwiches.

She ignored the clanging and banging of Kurt's operation on the engine. Once he swore crudely, which was unusual for him. She thought he'd hit his thumb, but she didn't ask. She didn't want to know.

Finally, the engine disappeared to its usual hidden location behind the passageway bulkhead. She was startled to hear it roaring to life a moment later, but decided Kurt was checking the results of whatever maintenance he'd been doing. Normally, she'd follow him into the cockpit and ask. Not today. Today she wasn't talking any more than she could help.

The boat was rocking gently from Kurt's motions up on deck. The engine was still running. Charging the batteries?

She had the counter washed and everything put away before she realised they were actually moving. She shot out, into the cockpit.

'Where are we going?' she demanded.

'Cumshewa. Take the wheel while I get the fenders up.' He was telling her, not asking her. He didn't wait for an answer, but walked away and left the wheel untended.

She couldn't leave the vessel unpiloted in such close waters. She told herself that was the only reason she'd moved to the wheel, guiding the vessel around the breakwater, to the right of the fishing boat steaming towards the floats.

Cumshewa was on the south island, probably the first decent anchorage if they were setting out on a cruise of the east coast of the Charlottes. But they weren't. Kurt had called Harriet and Brent yesterday. He'd be waiting for them to arrive before starting out from Queen Charlotte City.

And Dana didn't even know if she wanted to go with them.

If she could get her emotions sorted out, get back in control of herself, she might be able to decide whether two more articles were worth the price of being trapped on a forty-five-foot boat with Kurt while this fury existed between them.

Dana piloted them down the centre of the harbour, turning north towards Lawn Point. Kurt stood at the bow for a long time. She watched his tall, lean form from the cockpit, saw his fair hair blowing in the wind. She had put the steering on automatic, but she stayed at the wheel.

'Turn to the east now,' he shouted back at her. 'Right now!'

She had the autopilot off, was spinning the wheel. 'You're crossing the bar?'

'It's safe enough here. We have enough tide.'

Still it was a risk. You couldn't see the bar, and the sand shifted, didn't stay where the charts said it was.

'This is your risk,' she told him. 'I'm steering, but if we go aground, it's your responsibility.'

She was scared, crossing that stretch of water, taking that kind of chance, but Kurt just laughed and started past her to go below.

'We won't go aground. I've been talking to the fishermen, checking it out. Steer due east magnetic until we've gone three miles, then you can head south. I'm going down to find us some food.'

So he was talking to her again.

'I made salmon sandwiches—in the fridge—and salad.' Her own voice was cold. It was childish to hold her anger, but she couldn't—didn't want to feel any warmth.

Sounds good. Hungry, Dana? Shall I bring you some?'

She shook her head.

He brought a plate for them both, ignoring her denial of hunger. They ate the sandwiches together in the cockpit, silently, then worked together at putting up sails as they came clear of the shallows. The wind was perfect for their trip south. They sailed, brisk and close-hauled, past the airport and south for miles until they could turn into Cumshewa Inlet. When they turned, they let the sails far out and ran straight into the inlet on the wind.

There was a dock at the end of the inlet, and the masts of another boat, but Kurt steered left, into a small secluded bay that could have been a thousand miles from anywhere. When he had found the spot he wanted, he started the engine and put Dana back on the wheel while he went forward to drop the anchor himself.

When he signalled her to kill the engine, the sound faded quickly, absorbed by the trees on shore. He was still standing on the foredeck, didn't turn or move at all as she approached him.

'What about Harriet and Brent?'

'They won't be coming. Brent's in the throes of giving birth to a new whodunnit—he can't leave it.'

Kurt had listened to Harriet telling him this the night before, realising that everything was conspiring to put him alone with Dana. When Harriet hung up, he had been left with the hum of the empty wire, mentally scrabbling for other names, other friends to call.

What if he didn't call anyone else at all?

It wasn't love. Of course it wasn't love. They were friends. They could share warmth without it meaning love. He should have dialled the operator again, but with Dana waiting in the hotel dining room it suddenly seemed crazy to be looking for someone to protect him from her.

He had hung up the receiver and returned to the dining room, only to find Dana dancing in the arms of another man.

He'd turned away, talking to the others, seeing Dana without watching her. If he had walked up to them, cut in, he thought Dana would have gone with him.

He didn't. To do that would be staking a claim. He had no intention of staking a claim on any woman. Never again.

'They're not coming?'

'That's right.'

She looked around the bay, trying to assemble her reactions.

'And why did you sneak out of port without my knowing? What right have you to assume I even want to complete this trip now? After last night, I don't know that I want to spend the next few week alone with you!'

'Were not exactly in the middle of nowhere. That's Cumshewa over there. If you looked when we came in, you'd have seen boats, vehicles, a road. If you want to leave, I'll take you over in the dinghy when it's light.'

'I'll think about it.'

Kurt made supper. They ate in silence, then Dana refused a game of chess and went to her cabin, closing the door tightly behind her.

Some time in their last visit to Prince Rupert, Kurt had acquired a bag filled with pocket books—including a number of the crime novels he knew Dana loved to read. She had grabbed one of these at random on the way to her cabin, but it must have been one of the worst-written mysteries in the history of crime literature. The words made no sense, the sentences falling like separate stones on her mind, with no connection, no interest.

It was early when she slept. Very early in the morning when she woke.

Kurt was asleep, the vessel silent as she crept up on deck, slipped into the dinghy and rowed ashore.

It wasn't much of a beach in their little cove, but she walked on it, absorbing the silence.

She would get Kurt to row her to the dock when he woke, find someone to give her a lift to the airport. She'd looked at the chart the night before. They had sailed a long way, out around the headland, but by road it wasn't far back to the airport.

She hadn't much cash, but she had a credit card, so there would be no problem getting home. Her parents wouldn't question her unexpected arrival when she told them the tests were done, that the other guests had returned home and Dana had decided it was time she left, too. Her father would realise that she wasn't telling the whole story, but he would say nothing. Her mother would start looking for another man to fill the role of prospective son-in-law.

Dana would look for a job.

Her name would be mud in the publishing industry

when she failed to complete her contract for the last two articles. That series was a feather in her cap, could help her find a job somewhere in media. But, if she didn't finish it——

She found a rock and sat on it, chin in her hands, frowning at the sand.

It would satisfy her pride to walk out right now, walk away from Kurt—but it could do only harm to her career.

She knew Kurt was up when she saw the smoke rising from the stovepipe. He'd started a wood fire to disperse the early morning chill. Later, when the sun was high, he would let the fire go out.

Dana rowed the dinghy silently back. Kurt was standing on the deck, waiting for her. She passed the painter to him, refused the offer of his hand to help her climb up on to the deck.

'Breakfast's ready.'

Dana nodded. She'd smelled bacon frying as she docked the dinghy. She followed him down below.

She had no trouble eating. The lump of anger was gone, but she felt cold now—cold beyond shivering. She noted with a surprised satisfaction that it didn't matter that Kurt was across from her, watching her.

'Do you want me to take you in to Cumshewa?' he asked.

'I would say yes, except that I have a commitment to write two more articles. I'd damage my career if I broke that contract. I can't afford to do that.'

'So you're going on? Until we get back to Sointula?'

'Yes.'

'Then we should get under way.' They'd been taking their time all summer, exploring every bay that took their fancy. Now, Kurt moved as if they had a tight schedule to adhere to.

'I'll get us out of here,' he told her, moving away as he

talked. 'When you're finished washing up, make us a
new schedule—for both the watches and the galley.'

They had north winds for the next two days, ideal for
the course they were on. The engine remained silent as
Windflower II wove in and out of the complicated
network of inlets, working her way slowly southward.

They stopped to see the deserted Indian village at
Aero. They stopped in a bay called Rockfish Harbour
where they invited a couple aboard from a small kayak.
The Davidsons were exploring the island by kayak,
tenting ashore each night, enjoying their honeymoon.
They eagerly accepted an invitation for clam chowder
aboard Kurt's yacht, talking with a lively enthusiasm
that covered the coolness between Dana and Kurt.

When the evening ended, they stood on deck
together, waving as the Kayak moved silently towards
the shore.

Beside Dana, Kurt's low voice asked, 'Are you
determined to stay mad at me for ever?'

'I've every right to be angry. You were—you had no
right to talk to me like that, in Queen Charlotte.
You——'

'I know. I'm sorry.'

'Why did you——?'

'Can we just forget it, pretend it didn't happen? I'm
missing our games of chess. And conversation. With
everyone else gone, it seems only reasonable that we
should spend some time talking to each other.'

She laughed unwillingly. 'You're the sailor who
doesn't mind being alone. Who do you talk to when
you're by yourself in the midst of the Pacific Ocean?'

'I talk to myself, but your presence inhibits me from
carrying on a solo conversation.'

'I'll bet it does! If you start talking to yourself, I'm
swimming for shore.'

'I thought you would,' he said drily.

That night, they spread out the navigation charts, planning the remainder of the cruise. They traced routes along narrow channels, looked up anchorages in the Pilot, weighing one against the other. Watching Kurt as he bent over the books, Dana suspected that he enjoyed the planning almost as much as the cruise itself.

There was something magical about the night. They swung gently at anchor, protected from the wind and waves, secluded in their own world by the water surrounding the yacht. With the kerosene lanterns throwing a warm light over the charts, a fire burning in the wood stove, Dana felt a warm contentment, although she had no more illusions that she and Kurt could ever be lovers . . .

She wasn't on dry land, but she had her feet planted firmly under her now. In her mind, Kurt had been her lover, but it had never been anywhere but in her mind.

Only a dream. She was awake now.

He was intelligent and personable. She looked up and let herself admire his fair hair, the strong line of his jaw, the warmth of his blue eyes which reflected his own inner self. He was a nice man.

Friends. Certainly, they were friends. A much more comfortable relationship than the one she had been wishing for.

Kurt proved that he was good company in the days that followed, taking them through a fascinating collection of bays and inlets as they worked their way south.

At Lyell Island, Dana wondered about the smoke which seemed to indicate civilisation.

'Let's go and look, then,' said Kurt, and they spent a pleasant day at the isolated logging camp they found there. Kurt got the loggers talking and Dana sat back, listening, trying to remember everything because she hesitated to bring out her notebook and risk inhibiting the conversation.

It was another world—conversation covered a range of topics from the war being waged between environmentalists and the logging companies, to the best fishing holes for catching a big halibut. Kurt didn't even smile when halibut was mentioned, but he caught Dana's eye and she knew he was laughing inside. The lockers under the dinette seats were packed solid with jars of halibut.

Kurt was the perfect companion, always ready to change his plans to suit her whims, to stop and explore the signs of something interesting on shore.

When they arrived at Hot Spring Island, they set anchor on rocky bottom just offshore.

'Just a lunch anchorage,' said Kurt, looking in at the rootops peeping through the trees. 'We're far too exposed to anchor here overnight.'

Dana had the Pilot book open. 'Bathtubs, it says here. Claw-footed bathtubs filled with a constant stream of hot water. How on earth did they ever get them ashore? Do you think we can do laundry here?'

'We'd better. We won't see a laundromat until we get to Sointula.'

They packed the laundry into a bag and rowed ashore to find that it was true—the island was scattered with old bathtubs all filled and overflowing with steaming water from the hot pool on top of the hill. The young Haida Indian couple who were caretakers greeted them and waved them on up the hill for a hot bath.

The first two bathtubs had a shelter built over them.

'There's our washtub,' decided Kurt, emptying the laundry into one of the massive tubs. 'We'll let it soak while we have our baths. I'll go on up the hill and use the pool there.'

Dana stripped and climbed into the second tub.

Incredible luxury! She had never really realised before how wonderful a hot bath could feel, especially after their wild sail that morning.

She could turn her head and look out at the wild hillside, but she didn't. She was swearing off romantic fantasies these days. She giggled. Sharing a shelter with a tub of laundry might not be in the best of romantic tradition, but it was practical.

She scrubbed herself, then the clothes. She let the water out and put the big hose back into the tub to fill it again with clear, steamy water for rinsing the laundry.

'Are you dressed?' Kurt called out.

'Yes. Come on in.' There wasn't a door, just an opening, but he had stopped a few feet short of the shelter to be sure she was ready before he came in.

'Here, I'll do that: those jeans are stiff, hard to wring out.'

She watched him working over the wet clothing, wringing almost every drop of water out and packing it all back into the laundry bag.

Of course, she wasn't really in love with him, but if she ever did decide to fall in love again, she would look for a man like this. Most men would have left her with the laundry, labelling it women's work.

'What's wrong?' He was staring at her with amused enquiry.

'Nothing.' She had been staring at him, heaven knew what showing in her face. 'Nothing—I was just thinking.'

The laundry was heavier going back. They carried it together. The wind had shifted while they were bathing, rippling the water around the yacht. They sailed off their anchor, stealing silently away, waving to the couple who stood on shore watching them go.

They moored on Ramsey Island, only a few miles

away. There they hung the wet clothes out on the lines, turning Kurt's yacht into a floating clothes line, then rowing ashore to explore, taking wieners and marsh-mallows and planning a fire.

When dark came, their fire made a warm circle of light, sending flickering shadows into the trees.

'Let's go for a walk,' Kurt invited.

'I'm too lazy for walking. And it's too dark.'

'Nonsense! There's a moon. Once we get away from the firelight, we'll have plenty of light.'

'How can you have any energy after eating all those marshmallows? You—no, don't! Dana stumbled to her feet to avoid his long arm. 'I'm coming!'

Away from the fire, she found the path through the trees illuminated by a strong beam of moonlight.

'This way, Danish girl.' Kurt's voice was low, hardly disturbing the quiet. 'There's a beach through here.'

It was bathed in a soft light, a mile of golden sand stretching away in a smooth curve.

'Worth it?' he asked softly.

'Yes. Yes, of course.' A shell crunched under her foot, the only sound other than a gentle rushing from the surf. 'We have the world to ourselves.'

His hand brushed against hers as they walked, then they were walking silently, her smaller fingers lace through his, feeling the callouses he had developed from handling rope on the sails.

Friends could hold hands. It wasn't just for lovers.

'Do you know the stars?' he asked.

'Only a few. The Big Dipper—over there—and Polaris. When I look for the Little Dipper, I get confused.'

'Right there.' He turned her, lifting the hand that held hers to point.

'Which one? I can never tell?'

His hands slipped to her shoulders as he stood behind

her, his head against hers, his breath warm on her cheek as he pointed again. 'See?'

'Yes,' she whispered, somehow unable to find her normal voice, feeling him against her back, his breath sending a shiver along her spine. His hands slipped down, along her arms, moving softly until he grasped her wrists lightly.

'Has it been there all the time?' she asked him breathlessly. 'Hiding whenever I look?'

'Yes, of course. Turn around.' His hands urged her to face him, but she pulled away. She was suddenly cold, shivering where his hands had touched.

'I meant the stars,' she told him.

'I know what you meant.' The moon was too bright. Kurt could easily read whatever was in her face. She started walking again, pushing her hands into the pockets of her jeans.

'Dana?'

'Do you think the weather will be good for our crossing back to the mainland? The forecast——'

'Dana, that night—in Queen Charlotte—I had no right to——'

'Then why did you? I——'

'It would be easier to tell you if you would come here.'

She stepped away as he moved towards her. 'I don't think so.'

'Dana!' He laughed on an exasperated breath. 'I can't seduce you from five feet away!'

She stopped, startled.

'You—are you trying to seduce me? For goodness' sake, this isn't the sort of thing you talk about in cold blood! You—why?'

'You know why.' Kurt moved closer. His hands were on her shoulders again, drawing her against him. His head was blocking out the sky.

Her whole attention became focused on his lips

moving closer to hers. When he drew her body to rest against the length of his, she didn't resist, but let his mouth tease her lips apart.

'That's why,' he whispered as his lips drew slowly away from hers. She stared up at him, seeing his lips still parted from their contact with hers, hearing his breathing unsteady as he told her, 'Because I want you. You've known that for a long time.'

'How would I know that? You—what do you mean, want?'

'I don't think I'll ever be able to love anyone again, but you know as well as I the chemistry that's between us. There's no reason we can't——'

'You're asking me to be your mistress? A very temporary mistress?'

He laughed uncomfortably. 'That's an old-fashioned word, Dana. I just had to make it clear that I—well, that——'

'You're trying to say you don't love me. That you've no intention of ever falling in love with me. You make it sound a pretty cold-blooded proposition, Kurt.'

'Cold-blooded it's not.' He caught her against him and gave her a hard, quick kiss that reminded her of his angry kiss in the Hecate Strait.

For a moment she surrendered to his arms, feeling the emotions well up in her again, the overwhelming urge to be one with him.

'Kurt, I——'

'Hmm?' His lips found her ear and nibbled gently.

I love you, she had almost said. The last thing he wanted to hear.

'No,' she said instead, pushing her way out of his arms.

CHAPTER SEVEN

THEY went to see the sea-lions at the extreme southern tip of the islands, and visited yet another abandoned Indian village, with ruins of ancient totem poles still standing. One day they woke up and looked around at the pleasant anchorage they'd found, and simply stayed.

Dana baked bread that day, and Kurt changed the oil in the diesel engine. For most of the day they lazed about, reading books from the selection they'd picked up in Prince Rupert. Kurt read a science fiction novel, but Dana accused him of taking a vicious pleasure in picking holes in the author's theories. Dana got into a spy thriller, suspending belief as the hero sustained an incredible selection of injuries without losing his ability to devastate the enemy.

Kurt made no further mention of seducing her. She was relieved that the subject didn't come up again.

Or was she? Should she have said yes when she had the chance, hoping that Kurt would come to love her, despite his denials?

The wind died, then returned, but light and variable. They had two lazy days of sailing while the winds were deciding whether to blow. Dana finished the article on the Queen Charlottes the first day. The second day, they sailed into a small sound, then found the wind had totally disappeared. They set to work taking the sails down.

As Kurt was lowering the jib, the halyard jammed. It took the binoculars to confirm that it had caught at the top of the mast.

He played with the wire halyard for ten minutes or
so, jerking it and pulling it, hoping it would release.
Then he frowned and cursed and went back into the
lazarette hatch for the bo'sun's chair.

'I'll have to go up and release it,' he told Dana,
dropping a bundle of rope on to the deck with the
bo'sun's chair.

'How are you going to get up there?' There were steps
in the shrouds that went up to the first cross-arms, but
the halyard was jammed right at the top.

'You're going to hoist me up.' He was tying a line,
testing it.

'You've got to be kidding! I can't pull you up there!'

'We'll use the anchor winch. You don't need much
strength. Just don't let go.'

He arranged the lines, showed her how the line that
would lift him wrapped around the drum of the winch,
how she was to operate the winch and take up the slack
as it came off the drum.

Dana found it awkward, holding the line while she
levered the winch. She tried to shift her hands so that it
worked better, but she always came up feeling she
hadn't enough hands.

The line started to creak as it took Kurt's weight.

'You're sure this rope is strong enough? You're
heavy——'

'Not that heavy. The breaking strength of this stuff is
twelve hundred pounds. Just keep going until I tell you
to stop.'

She wrapped the line around her hand again, then
glanced back at him. He was suspended in the chair a
couple of feet above the deck, one arm thrown around
the mast, ready to be pulled up. She turned back,
worked the winch again, pausing to untangle the line.
Every time she had to shift her grip, she had a vision of
it getting away from her, of Kurt falling to the deck

from the top of the mast.

'Keep going, Dana. It's fine.'

It wasn't fine at all. She was terrified, knew that she could not trust herself for this job, that she couldn't risk Kurt's life.

Letting him down was easier. She let the line slide slowly on the drum, holding it with both of her hands, controlling his descent until she heard his feet touch the deck. Then she let go.

'What's wrong?'

'I'm sorry, but I can't do it. I could work the winch, or I could tail the rope, but I can't do both. I can't get the hang of it, and I'm afraid I'll lose my grip on the rope. If there was a second person here, to help me——'

'Well, there isn't.' He climbed out of the chair, looking up, frowning.

'Will it take much strength to get it unjammed?'

'I doubt it, but it takes someone up there to do it. Look, I'll run the rope differently, around the jib winch too, and you'll just have to——'

'No. I'll go up,' she said suddenly.

'What?'

'You said it wouldn't take that much strength. All right, I'll go up. You pull me up the mast. I'll get the wire unjammed.'

'You can't go up there.'

'Why not?'

'That mast is fifty-feet high. Once you get up to the top, there's not much to hang on to. It can be pretty frightening.'

She considered the mast. 'I didn't realise it was that high, but it doesn't make much difference, does it? The rope is strong enough—you said that—and it makes a lot more sense for me to go up. I'm a lot lighter than you, and you're stronger. You might even be able to pull me up without using the winch, so you'd have both hands for the rope.'

'I don't like it. A woman——'

'Come on, Kurt, you're not a chauvinist! It doesn't make sense. Going up there isn't he-man stuff. It just takes a head for heights, and I do have that. At this end, handling the rope, that's the part that takes the muscles. And I'm used to working in a bo'sun's chair. I've helped Dad paint the light-tower every year since I was seventeen, you know.'

She was already in the bo'sun's chair, ready for him to pull her up. 'Tell me what I have to do when I get to the top. And give me some hints on going up—how will I get around the cross-arms?'

He checked every knot and fastening on both the chair and the rope, tied the tools she might need to the chair, so she wouldn't have to think about hanging on to them, showed her how to fasten the safety line around the mast.

'It's perfectly safe,' he told her, 'as long as you keep the safety line on. I wouldn't let you go up there if it weren't safe, but it can be frightening.'

The lines across his forehead were deep. He didn't want to let her go, but had no good reason to stop her. 'You have to undo the safety line when you get to the cross-arms. Any time you want me to stop, just tell me. If you're frightened, just tell me and I'll bring you back down. We can go back to Lyell Island and find a couple of strong men to haul me up.'

Dana shook her head. If Kurt tried to sail all the way to Lyell Island with the jib half raised, he'd surely tear the sail beyond repair with the first strong wind they encountered.

'I'll be all right,' she insisted. 'I'm not going to look down, and I'll be very careful.'

He raised her easily, smoothly and slowly, until she called to him.

'I'm at the first cross-arm.'

She unsnapped the safety line, holding herself in close to the mast with a tight grip on a shroud while she got the safety line above the cross-arm. She felt a sudden awareness of her height above the deck in the moment before she snapped the line back around the mast.

'Okay now! Go ahead,' she called down.

'You're sure you're all right?' He was talking quietly so that his voice would not startle her.

'I'm fine.'

The second cross-arm was a little more difficult. There was less to hang on to and the mast moved more at this height. When the vessel rode gently on an almost invisible swell, the upper part of the mast swung through an arc of a foot or more.

'Stop a minute!' she called down during one such wild swing, when she couldn't seem to find anything to hold on to to keep herself against the mast. The higher she got, the fewer handholds there were.

'Do you want me to bring you down?' called Kurt.

'No, I'm almost there. I have to figure this out. Will you pull me up about six more inches, then stop?'

It was a precarious feeling, perched at the top of the mast. She wasn't foolish enough to look down, but with the horizon all around her she couldn't help knowing where she was. There was nothing on her level to look at except the fitting on the top of the mast. She stared intently at that.

'You're tied off,' Kurt told her quietly. 'So you're quite secure. Can you see the jammed wire?'

'Yes. If you can let the halyard go slack, I think I can just lift it back into the track. There's a pin that's meant to keep the wire from coming out, but it's worked loose.'

She worked slowly, hampered by the need to hang on.

'Okay! You can let me down!' she called finally.

Kurt lowered her slowly, stopping at intervals, until she was back on the deck.

'Are you all right?' He was helping her out of the bo'sun's chair, divesting her of rope and tools as if she were unable to do even the smallest thing for herself. 'Are you sure you're okay?'

'I'm fine. Really, I'm fine, Kurt. Stop fussing!'

He stepped back and frowned at her. 'Why, you witch! I believe you enjoyed that daredevil stunt you just pulled!'

Dana laughed. 'Well, I suppose I did. It was scarey up there, but there's something about it. It's stimulating!'

He had hold of her by the shoulders. He bent down and gave her a hard, almost angry kiss, then had stepped back from her before she had time to respond in any way.

'Here I am, pulling you up and worrying that you're going to pass out from terror, and all the while you're getting some perverse kick out of it! Come on, let's put these lines away and sail over to that inlet. You may be fine, but I'm not. After watching you up there, I need an early anchorage and a long, lazy evening to recover!'

Not fair, she told him silently. With that half-angry kiss he had evidently got rid of his own feelings of anger and frustration at being inactive below while she climbed the mast. His forehead was smoother now, his eyes almost laughing. But with his brief embrace he had set her heart pounding hard in her breast. In just seconds, he had totally destroyed her illusion of having gained a relative immunity to his attraction for her.

It was her day to cook, but he wouldn't let her do anything except relax in a deckchair. He made dinner

for her and served it on deck. Strangely, after the
zinging high she had felt on coming down the mast, she
felt suddenly weak and exhausted.

There was just enough wind to keep the flies away.
They watched the sun set from the canvas deck chairs
after Kurt had cleared away the last of their supper.

'The dishes,' she reminded him as they sat sipping
coffee. 'I should go down and start the dishes.'

'They'll keep.'

So they sat in silence as the day seeped away,
watching the stars appear slowly over the trees. The
silence was easy, intimate. Dana felt there was nothing
that she could not ask Kurt.

'Kurt?'

'Hmm?' He had leaned back in the chair to get a
better view of the stars.

'Do you still miss her very much?'

Somewhere, a night owl hooted. Overhead, a sound
that might have been a high-passing jet.

It's not so simple as that, Dana.' His hand grasped
hers in the dark, and he held it. His thumb rubbed
gently against the back of her hand. 'Three years is a
long time, you've said. Yet, when Celeste and Patricia
died in that fire, I don't think I really knew what had
happened. For a long time I was numb. Of course, I
knew they were gone, I was living alone, but—you
know how it is when you know something with your
mind, but not with your heart?
I'd come home—it wasn't even the same place we'd
lived together in, but I'd expect them to be there. I
wouldn't even realise it until I found myself alone in an
empty apartment.

'I felt as if I'd see them, any minute, just around the
corner. I'd be walking downtown and catch sight of
someone who looked—just for a moment—as if——'

'As if it were Celeste? Like me, on the deck in Bishop Bay.'

He squeezed her hand. 'That night was a much more tangible fantasy. In Montreal, in the year after the fire, I don't think I was really sane. Andy—Andy's dad— suggested a boat, trying to get me out of the slump, I think. In the end, I started building this boat, not so much because I wanted to, as to try to get myself—my life—under control again. Sailing was a part of my life that Celeste had never shared, so it was neutral, a place where the ghosts could leave me alone.'

Not always. Celeste's ghost had been strong and close to him the night he made love to Dana on the deck.

'I knew I wouldn't marry again, that I wasn't going to fall in love again. Love makes you so terribly vulnerable, Dana. Once—once in a lifetime is enough for a risk like that. A few times, there were women. It wasn't any good. I had physical needs, but whenever I was with a woman, Celeste was still there too, and I felt—I couldn't help feeling I was being unfaithful to her.'

'Were you trying to pretend?' she asked softly. 'Like you did with me?'

'Yes, that too. You haven't hesitated to tell me a few home truths. I've had to admit to a lot of what you said that night in Prince Rupert. For a long time, Celeste was still alive for me. Then, after that, she was gone, but I was still hanging on to her memory, maybe as a kind of protection from life, and because—we were happy, and I've missed her.

'You're the first woman I've really wanted since I lost Celeste, and I resented that. I couldn't help feeling that every time I touched you, Celeste was slipping further away.'

'I don't go out with married men, Kurt.' Her voice

was clear on the night air. 'I don't think, in the beginning, that I really understood that you were still married.'

'Is that why you said no to me the other night?'

'I suppose. Partly. And partly—because you put it in words, I guess. It seemed such a cold proposition—an affair, just for the rest of the trip. It puts me in the same category as a disposable flashlight, doesn't it?'

'Can't we share something less than a major commitment?'

'Perhaps, Kurt, but not like that—as if it's a business transaction.'

'Dana, you're such a direct person yourself—how can you be offended by plain speaking? It had to be in words. I couldn't take a chance that you might misunderstand what I was offering.'

'There was no misunderstanding.' He was offering everything but love—closeness without giving himself. 'It's cold, don't you think, now that the sun has set? I think I'll go down and wash up.'

He didn't stop her. She took his cup and got to her feet.

'I'll put the chairs away,' he told her. 'And—Dana?'

'Yes?'

'That was quite a job you did today, going up that mast!'

She laughed. 'Impressed you, did it?'

'Damned right, it did!'

She was still smiling over that when the dishes were done.

Kurt must have thought she looked tired, for when he came in to help dry dishes, he sent her off to bed for the night.

She slept restlessly, waking in the dark. She didn't turn on the light, but lay quietly, listening. She could see a light glimmering through the ventilation holes over her door. Moments later, she heard sounds.

Kurt, getting up, pouring himself a cup of coffee, settling down again.

Then quiet. He would be reading, sipping his coffee.

Dana knew she had dreamed of Kurt. Not a fantasy dream. A vague shadowy dream that had probed his loss, his loneliness.

Now, in the night, she remembered the days after her father's accident, the fear of loss. As a child, she had had a deep belief in the immortality of her father. Her mother hadn't. She remembered a long wait with her mother, in a hospital room, her mother quiet and still and deathly pale—holding herself stiff and separate from everyone around.

Her mother would understand how Kurt felt.

They would be back at Sointula in a few days. The long sail across the open water, then they'd be back on Vancouver Island—almost home . . . almost parting.

She got silently out of her bunk. She stripped of her flannel pyjamas and replaced them with a short, silky nightgown. Not the gown she had worn the night Kurt mistook her for Celeste; this gown was black and brief, clinging to her curves, ending at mid-thigh. Theoretically, it was more modest than a bathing suit.

Dana stood uncertainly for a moment, then opened the door and slipped out of her cabin.

He was in the salon, reading by the light of a kerosene lantern. He could have turned on the electrics, but she knew he preferred the warm flicker of the lantern.

He watched her as she stood in her doorway, looking across at him. She found she was breathless, suddenly nervous.

'Hello?' The book was in his lap. His mug was on the counter beside him. 'Couldn't you sleep?'

She had no words to answer him. She crossed the

floor silently in her bare feet, sitting a few inches away from him on the settee.

'Dana?' He touched her hair, brushed a strand back from her face. 'Are you all right?'

'Yes.' She closed her eyes as his fingers moved softly in her hair. 'I didn't think I'd be nervous, but I am.'

'Are you?' Kurt put his book aside, turned so that he could face her. With both hands, he lifted her long hair back from her face. 'You needn't be,' he whispered softly.

She sat silently as he took her face in his hands, feeling its contours gently with his roughened fingers. When his hands drifted down to her bare shoulders, the warm tide ran up in her, flushing her skin.

'Have you changed your mind?' she whispered.

'No.' He touched her lips with his, gently so that a shiver went through her thinly-clothed body. 'I'm hoping you've changed yours.'

His hands slid across the silk on her back, drawing her closer. She went, sliding into the warmth that was his arms around her, his lips on hers. Her head was cradled against his shoulder and he brushed her lips gently, then more firmly as her own mouth trembled under his.

She opened her lips to him. His tongue explored the soft, sensitive areas of her mouth. She reached up her arm, lacing her fingers into his hair, bringing her body closer to his.

His hand on her back was warm, probing the hollow along her spine, holding her close. His other hand moved, tracing the curves from her shoulder, along her silky back, her hip, and down to where his fingers brushed the soft skin of her outer thigh. He slipped his arm under her legs, lifting her up so that her legs lay across his.

'That's better,' he murmured, 'now I can hold you closer.'

His lips had left hers, were tracing the shape of her temple. His free hand smoothed the hair back. Her head nestled comfortably against his shoulder. The slow motion of his fingers slid through her long hair, gently pulling her head back, temporarily soothing the fever that was rising in her.

'I love your hair,' he told her, smoothing it until her head was tipped back and her neck exposed to him. She met his eyes and saw a smoky desire in them—no memories, no ghosts. Then he bent down to trail a kiss along her neck and back to her lips.

His hand left her hair to move along her shoulder, to slide down across the roundness of a full breast. She shuddered in his arms and gripped his head with both hands. His hair tangled through her fingers as she pulled his mouth to hers.

'You're beautiful.' He had to be talking about feeling, not seeing, because his eyes were closed as his words brushed her lips. He bent closer, taking her lips in a deep, intimate kiss.

When his mouth left hers she was trembling, dizzy, her lips seeking after his, not wanting to let them move away yet. She moved her body against him until his arms gripped her hard, holding her closer, crushing her softness against him as he took her lips again.

Then his mouth trailed down her throat, to the sensitive hollow at its base, then further, burning the curve of her breast through her nightgown.

'Come here, Dana.' He drew her to her feet, sliding his arms behind her, bending to kiss her again.

She held his hand as he led her into his cabin. She sank down in the big double berth, waiting until he came to her.

He leaned over her, his hands tracing down,

moulding the soft fullness of her through the silk. His fingers found the aroused peaks of her breasts, squeezing gently. He watched her intently through darkly heated eyes as he touched her, watching for her eyes to close and her head to drop back as his caresses sent a wave of weakness through her.

'Kurt——'

'What, Dana?' He'd found the smooth thrust of her hip, the long length of her thigh with its soft, sensitive inner surface. 'You're so beautiful.'

Love me, she wanted to say. I love you.

'I need you,' she whispered, finding her hands on his chest, feeling the taut hardness of him.

CHAPTER EIGHT

DANA woke to find Kurt's body curled against her back, his arm across her hip. She closed her eyes again, savouring his closeness. He shifted once, mumbling something incomprehensible as his arm drew her back against him possessively.

If she could wake like this, with Kurt near, every day——

She mustn't let herself think those thoughts. There were only a few days, so very few.

She turned so that she could see him, afraid of waking him, afraid waking would be when they parted, separated by the activities of the day.

His hair was tousled across his forehead. She had done that, last night. She remembered the feeling of her hands in his hair. She touched gently, smoothing back the unruly locks.

His face was younger in sleep, more vulnerable. She stared at him for long moments, then touched the corner of his mouth gently. When she came closer to him, slipping her arms around him, his arms tightened on her. Her head was on his shoulder. She found herself staring at the fine hairs on his chest.

Her hands were fascinated by the feel of him, the smooth skin with the ripple of muscle below. She touched his shoulder, the contours of his chest, the tautness of his stomach. She traced a scar from surgery. She must ask him about that.

'That's one hell of a way to wake up, Danish girl,' he growled, imprisoning her with his arms, drawing her

close against him. Her hair fell in a wild cloud across
his chest.

'Good morning,' she said as he wove his fingers
through her hair and brought her lips to his.

He kissed her deeply, slipping his hands down along
her back, down to her thighs, tracing the curves of her
as he moulded her feminine body against his. Her heart
was pounding hard, the world spinning. She closed her
eyes, gave herself up to the pleasure of his touch.

'I was dreaming about you,' he told her in a low
voice, his lips tracing a path towards her neck. 'I
dreamed this Danish girl was waking me up, making
love to me. She touched me . . .' he took her hand to
show her, 'here . . . and here . . .'

She touched him, stirring his hands and his mouth to
passion. Then he gripped her in his arms and took her
where there were no words, driving her body to a frenzy
in his arms, taking her to the edge of the world . . . and
back.

In the dizzy aftermath of their passion, he held her in
his arms, stroking her, caressing her gently as their
breathing slowly returned to normal.

They slept, together, the sun beating through the
porthole as morning passed. Outside, the sea-birds
moved overhead. A fishing boat steamed past in the
channel, its skipper looking in at the sailboat lying at
anchor, wondering . . .

When she woke again, Dana was alone in the bunk.

She lay still, listening to the sounds of Kurt in the
galley. She could smell coffee and the aroma of bacon
frying.

Had he watched her sleeping?

Earlier, she had lain awake in his arms, wanting
every moment of closeness, not wanting to leave him
even though he wasn't awake.

He obviously hadn't felt the same. He had left her,

got up to start his day alone.

Her nightgown was lost somewhere in the tumbled
bedding. A short bathrobe of Kurt's hung on a hook
near the door. She belted it around her, wondering if
he'd mind. She could smell traces of his aftershave on
the robe. Wearing it seemed to Dana an intimate
gesture, slightly daring.

'That you, Dana?' Kurt's voice, from the galley. He
met her as she came out into the passageway, a fork in
his hand. He was smiling, bending to kiss her cheek.
'Coffee?'

'Love some.' She would rather have thrown her arms
around him, told him how she loved him, but his lips
were cool as they touched her cheek. Affectionate, but
cool.

'Have a good sleep?' He expertly lifted the bacon
from the pan and cracked two eggs into it.

'Very good. Would you like me to take over making
breakfast?'

'No. Go ahead and get dressed while I finish. Two
eggs for you all right? Once we've eaten we'll get under
way.'

In her own cabin she dressed quickly. Kurt's voice
had been brisk, his mind already on the day's journey.

'Will we start the crossing today?' she called back to
him.

'I think so—there, your breakfast's ready—the
weather report looks good. North-west winds for the
next forty-eight hours. Perhaps we'll sail right over to
Bull Harbour.'

Bull Harbour. That was the northern tip of Vancouver Island, almost home. Dana tucked her blouse in.
She usually wore it loose. When she tucked it in, it
emphasised the fullness of her breasts, the curve of her
waist and hip.

'How long will that take?' she asked through the

door, staring at her own reflection in the mirror.

'Depends on the wind—if we start out now, perhaps we'd be in by tomorrow at sunset. If the wind drops, it could take another day.'

In the mirror, her face was bleak. She smoothed her fingers across it, making a mask for Kurt to see. Vancouver Island tomorrow night. Two more days to Sointula—one day if he wanted to hurry.

'Coming, Dana? Your food's getting cold.'

'Half a minute.'

She applied a light coating of lipstick with shaking hands, then she got her smile firmly in place and went out to eat her breakfast.

She had to keep it cool. It would be so easy to lose control of herself. If she let herself, she'd be clinging to Kurt, begging him to take her with him—to Montreal, the South Pacific, anywhere at all.

It wouldn't be any good—she knew that. Last night, in her arms, she thought he'd been with her at the ends of the world. This morning, when she woke him, he had been dreaming of her. She could have told him she would be in his dreams for ever, but it wouldn't have been true.

There had been passion, and certainly there was affection, but this morning Kurt Saunders was thoroughly in control. Last night hadn't thrown him off his stride, wasn't even slowing down his journey by as much as a day.

Dana was in control too. She made sure of that. She had a few days left, but she couldn't afford the luxury of letting herself go.

She washed the dishes while Kurt brought the anchor up. Then she went around below decks, putting things away, making sure cabinet doors were shut. She made Kurt's bed, found her nightgown buried in the tumbled bedding and put it away in her own cabin.

Land was all around them when she came up on deck.

'Everything's shipshape, Kurt. I've checked the hatches, put everything away.'

'Good. We'll be in the open in another hour. We'll have the wind on our quarter, so it probably won't be rough, but maybe you could make a thermos of coffee, just in case.'

'I did that. And sandwiches.' If the winds increased, they would want handy food and coffee without the risk of cooking in rough water.

'I should have known you would.' His smile was approving. 'Find yourself a corner and relax, why don't you? You've earned it.'

She mustn't crowd him, mustn't stay too close when he didn't want her near. She went down for her book, then settled on the deck where she was protected from the wind.

She could look up from her book and see him, watch him as he stood at the wheel, a sailor's cap on his head to shield his eyes from the sun. She had an album of pictures of Kurt stored in her memory, but she needed more, to keep her through the years ahead.

The winds were with them as they came into the open. They set full sail and raced through the open water, keeping the same tack all through the afternoon. When Dana turned the last page of her book, she hardly knew who the murderer was, but she knew she had to get active, do something.

'The skylight needs varnishing, doesn't it?' She had been leaning against the oak frame to the big skylight as she read. 'I could sand and varnish it.'

'You could sand it. We'd have to leave the varnishing until we're out of the wind. If you want to do it, I'll get out the supplies.'

In the end they did it together. Kurt set the windvane

steering, then got out sandpaper. They worked together as the yacht sailed herself steadily across the open water.

It was harder work than she would have expected, sanding the old varnish off, bringing the wood to a smooth perfection with fine sandpaper. After a while she sat back to rest, watching Kurt work on steadily.

'You've almost finished the articles?' She could tell from his voice that he wasn't out of breath at all. He had worked more steadily then her, not expending everything in the first burst of energy.

'Almost. I'm just starting the last one now. The first one should be on the stands when you get back to Vancouver.'

He was sanding the far corner of the skylight, carefully avoiding scratching the surface of the glass.

'What will you be doing when the trip's over? Will you be going back to Vancouver?'

She picked up the sandpaper again, rubbing the wood with a slower motion, imitating Kurt's rhythm. 'Not back to my old job. I'll spend some time at the lighthouse, working on getting some commentaries ready. Warren was pretty enthusiastic about the scripts I sent him. I'll be recording a whole series on costal anchorages.'

'And after that?'

What difference did it make what she did once he was gone?

'There's a radio job coming up. Warren said I'd have a good chance at it—a reporting job in the news department. I have my journalism degree, and the freelance work I've done for them already, plus this series for the magazine—I've a good chance.'

'So I'll turn on my radio and hear you reading the news one day?' The lines of his face deepened in a frown. 'Are you sure, Dana? Somehow, I don't see you chasing the news, meeting other people's deadlines, interviewing people who don't want to talk to you. You need a little more peace in your life than you'd get in a radio news department.'

The trouble was, he was right. She found the hectic pace of the radio station stimulating when she went to record her commentaries, but she knew it wasn't her kind of place. Not all day, every day. She needed the chance to be on her own, needed a quiet background to recharge her batteries for the more hectic moments in life.

'What I really want to do is write a book, but I need a job too. I've got this terrific idea for a mystery—a murder mystery on board a yacht.

'Tell me,' he encouraged her.

She had characters, and a situation. It had been growing in her mind over the last few weeks. It was a big project, but the passengers on this fantasy yacht were really taking shape. Telling Kurt about them was almost as if they had stepped on to the deck with them.

'What a surprising woman you are, Dana.' Kurt touched her hair. Her hair seemed to fascinate him. So often, when he was near, he reached to touch it. I'll never cut it, she vowed. Some day, Kurt might sail back into her life.

'Do I surprise you?' she asked him.

'Every day. Climbing my mast, sailing the dinghy heeled over to the rails—I bet you were a sucker for a dare when you were a kid.'

'I was,' she admitted. 'I used to get myself into such jams. When I was five I was dared to jump off the high diving board. I was terrified, but I had to go up.'

'I bet you went back up a second time, just to prove you weren't afraid.'

She laughed. 'It really wasn't so scarey the second time.'

'I can see you, a real little daredevil.'

'And you?' She caught his hand as it left her hair. 'You weren't a daredevil, were you? Of course, you've taken risks, crossed oceans, but——'

'Calculated risks,' he told her. 'Before I took a chance, I always wanted to be pretty sure I'd survive it.'

Like taking a chance on love. He had done that once. It hadn't seemed that much of a risk, falling in love with Celeste. Today, he knew that if he found Celeste on that beach in Bermuda, he'd be more wary. Opening his life to her had made him far too vulnerable to hurt.

Right now there was a very real danger. He had fooled himself, thinking he could simply choose not to love again. He had almost lost control of himself last night. Touching, holding, feeling her against him— he'd almost started saying words that shouldn't be said. He had certainly been thinking thoughts that shouldn't be in his mind—early this morning, when he'd woken needing her more than he could ever remember needing food or water.

Later, when he woke again, he had forced himself to get out of his bed, away from the temptation of Dana's sleeping body and the sight of her creamy soft skin. He had wanted to hold her close, to drown in her arms.

Even now he couldn't stop the images in his mind when he looked at her. She was covered with clothing and dust from the sanding, but all he could think of was throwing the rudder over and taking the sails aback to stall the ship. Then he'd take her in his arms, push the clothes aside and touch her.

If he touched her, excited her, she would begin to make love to him. Imagining it, thinking of the discovery of Dana's passionate nature last night, his hand tightened on hers, pulled her against him.

She was such a soft firmness. He let his eyes close as his lips touched hers, as his hands traced the firmness of her arms, then the softness of her breasts. He could feel every tremor of her skin, knew the excitment of his own hands on her as if he could share her mind.

He was learning the touch of her, knew how to bring the soft gasp from her throat. She was so different, this fair Danish girl. When he pushed her blouse away and found the beginning of her white softness with his lips, her hands came to him, returning his passion with her own.

Just one gentle kiss, a moment's closeness—he had deluded himself with that thought. His hand fumbled on the clasp of her bra as if he were a young boy touching a woman for the first time. Then his head moved down to the creamy softness and he kissed the rosy peak of one tempting breast, driving her wild in his arms with the touch of his tongue.

A part of him, separate, watching, knew the moment when she lost control, when her hands gripped him convulsively and she told him words of love—words he couldn't admit to hearing, even as they inflamed him beyond any chance of self-control.

Later, he held her exhausted body in his arms and tried to still his own trembling. Somewhere he found enough of his sanity to make his hands draw her blouse back into place, get himself away from her arms. There had been a moment when he might have begged her to stay with him to the ends of the world. Somehow, that desperate need had passed, but he knew that he could not risk touching her again.

'I think you should go below, Danish girl,' he told her when words were possible again. 'We'll be sailing overnight. You'll need sleep before you relieve me.'

He couldn't look at her as he spoke. He knew his sudden withdrawal, the coldness in his voice would hurt her. He looked up to see the jib quivering in the wind. He uncleated the jib sheet and pulled hard on it until the sail had stopped its vibration. When he took his hands from the line, they had stopped shaking.

It was easier once she was gone. He knew she was only a few steps away, yet he could tend to the ship. Moments ago, they'd been sailing without a captain or crew. Kurt was a careful, thorough captain, but he'd almost lost control of his whole world in those soft arms. Luckily, there'd been no hazards, only open ocean. He didn't know if he would have been aware of danger, if anything could have stopped their loving once he had her in his arms.

Not loving.

He mustn't use that word, even in his mind.

He sought the therapy of his chores, putting the sandpaper away, adjusting the trim of the sails. The wind was good—behind them, though perhaps a few knots lighter than he would have chosen.

He decided that changing the jib would be worthwhile—there was no sign of change in the sky. There would continue to be light winds. He pulled down the working jib, working with a harness as he always did when he was alone on deck. He ran the big genoa up, catching the light wind and picking up their speed by a full knot. By the time he had the sails changed and the whole thing logged, he had almost convinced himself he was alone on board.

He didn't wake Dana when her watch came. He was awake, alert, ready to stand watch through the whole night. It wouldn't be the first time.

In the slow hours of the night, when he might have been tempted to sleep, he brought out a pad and started sketching, working out installation configurations for various autopilot options. The better he prepared his paperwork, the less likelihood of his having to leave some South Pacific cruising haven for a flying trip to

Montreal to consult with a bewildered installation technician.

Of course he couldn't foresee every possible variable. There would be trips back to Canada, but he wanted to keep them to a minimum.

After spending the next few weeks in Montreal, he knew he would have had more than his fill of cities.

Where would Dana be when he came back to take *Windflower II* cruising again? Would she be city-bound again, caught in Vancouver to make a living? He wanted her to escape that, to free herself from the city he believed was foreign to her. She should——

He wouldn't see her again. Only days ago, he'd been thinking it might be possible to keep contact. Even letters might give him some feeling of her warmth. If he kept in touch he could close his eyes and see her, know she was doing well.

But if he wrote, then one day he would come closer, just to see her. There would be no end to the need, the wanting that could grow from letting her have even a small part of his life. Even here, alone on deck, he couldn't get away from her. She had filled the only part of his life that had always remained separate from others.

The line on his paper didn't relate to any installation he could conceive of. He tore the top sheet off, drew again carefully. Through the remainder of the night, he managed to keep his mind firmly entangled in theoretical lines and problems that had nothing to do with love or with tall, passionate Danish girls.

Dana brought him coffee with the dawn. He had heard her stirring, seen the smoke drifting out of the chimney from the wood fire she started. He was ready when she came, smiling with cool warmth to keep her away from his touch.

'Breakfast,' he suggested. 'I've lost track of our

schedule, but if you could make me a light breakfast, I'd fall into a deep sleep.'

'You're tired,' she scolded him gently. 'You should have woken me.'

'I'm fine. Just bring me breakfast, please, then I'll let you have the watch while I sleep.' He kept his eyes away from her, kept his hands busy so they could not think of touching her.

He had tired himself enough that he had no trouble falling asleep. He dropped the heavy curtain over his porthole and sank into the mattress, aware from the coolness of the sheets that when Dana went below to sleep, she had not come to his bed.

The heat of day had passed when he woke. He opened his eyes, knowing from the way the sun angled in his porthole that it was early evening. The boat hardly moved—riding at some sheltered anchorage, he realised. The hynotising motion of the Pacific swell was gone.

In his dreams, he had sailed on through that Pacific swell. He closed his eyes tightly, trying to push back the vivid picture of Dana sharing his dream journey. His mind probed some characteristic of the silence around him.

He was alone on board.

He pulled on his jeans, leaving his chest bare. He dashed up on deck, looking around, not recognising anything he saw, then spotting the dinghy pulled up on the beach a few hundred feet away.

He had panicked for a moment, realising she wasn't on board. He could see her now, walking on the beach. Of course, he'd been a little worried, as he might have been for any passenger.

She was the only passenger he'd ever had who had brought him into harbour while he slept. He'd never had a man on board who he would trust with his ship as he did Dana.

He went back below for his shirt. When he looked in the ship's log, he found that she had anchored them in a sheltered bay on the northern end of Vancouver Island. He'd slept the day away, not the mere four hours he had intended.

He checked their position against the chart, hardly surprised to discover Dana had anchored on the flat bottom, in the most secure part of the bay. When he got down to the galley he found coffee in a thermos on the counter.

He took the thermos with him when he heard her oars in the water, her voice calling,

'Ahoy! Can I ferry you in to shore? Beautiful beach here—clams, too, if you care to dig.'

She was sitting in the dinghy, looking up at him, smiling but with a faint uncertainty in her eyes. During the day, she must have had a lot of sun. Her face was flushed with a faint layer of sunburn over her tan. Kurt wanted to tell her she should keep a hat on in the hot sun. He said nothing at all. He passed down the shovel and thermos, then took the oars from her and returned the little dinghy to shore.

'Clam chowder would be good,' he agreed, keeping his eyes on the trees behind her as he rowed.

There weren't as many clams as they expected.

'Enough for breakfast tomorrow,' Dana declared.

She walked up the hard beach while he put the bucket of clams in the dinghy. When he came back, he found her standing in the midst of a complex drawing she was creating in the sand.

'Recognise it?' She was frowning down at a jagged line. 'How should this part be, Kurt? Does that little bit go out like this? Or——'

'Like this.' He took the stick from her and made

another line over hers. 'I take it this is a map of the west coast?'

'From Alaska to Panama,' she agreed, 'with some major inaccuracies, I'm sure.'

He considered her artwork. 'Not bad for an impromptu effort. It'll disappear when the tide comes in.'

'It's a blackboard for you—I'm sure this bit is wrong. How does the coast of Mexico go?'

'What do you mean, a blackboard?' He bent down to rub out the offending section of Mexico and redraw it.

'That's better. I knew I had it wrong—I'm working on the last article, but the endings wrong. There's only one way to end it—with a hint of what's next for Kurt Saunders and his ship. I know you're going to Montreal to get production going, but the readers are going to want to know about the next sea trip—after all, it's a sailing magazine.'

Kurt found a comfortable corner of a large rock to sit on. 'I suppose you're right.'

Dana nodded. Her eyes had the faraway look that told him she was visualising some idea in print. 'Tell me about the trip.' Her eyes were back on him now, direct and insistent. 'You'll be back for the floating boat show in winter, then what? You'll be getting ready to go sailing? Tell me about it, so I can get the picture, so I can leave the readers wondering, interested.'

'I haven't planned it all, Dana.' He was inexplicably alarmed at the thought of telling her his plans for when she was gone.

'Of course you have,' she insisted. 'Not exact dates and places, perhaps, but you've thought of it. This isn't a schedule, an itinerary you're giving me, just a picture. Here's the coast. There's Vancouver, where you'll start. Take me on a fantasy journey. Show me how the trip would be, so I can get the feel of it for the article.'

The first time he'd seen that look of dedicated insistence on her face had been at the lighthouse, as she persuaded him to take her aboard. Again, this time, he knew that she would have her way in the end.

He opened his hand to accept the stick from her, leaned down to make a mark where Vancouver would be.

'I can't just hop aboard and go,' he told her, marking the place where he would berth. 'She'll be in Anderson's marina, about here. When the boat show is over, I'll have a lot of work to get ready. She's not outfitted for deep sea cruising.' He started to list the jobs he knew must be done, the supplies he would need.

'That'll take a good three months, outfitting her and making sure everything's ready. Then, when she's ready, I thought of going out here.' He traced the route through Juan de Fuca Strait. 'I could take it in easy stages, down the coast to San Francisco, then,' he drew a line west, 'to Hawaii. I haven't gone that way before. We could sail south, to the islands—South Sea Islands—could spend a long time cruising them.' We? Had he said we?

He extended the map, tracing a route through a multitude of islands, filling the beach with a fantasy trip.

'I can see it,' she told him, following every curve of the line, asking the questions he knew she would ask. 'I can see you there.'

He stared down at the map they had made in the sand for a long moment. He could see all too clearly—not Kurt alone, but Dana with him, at his side.

'I'll take you back now,' he told her abruptly. 'The sun's setting. You'll be cold in that thin blouse.'

She was silent, sensing his withdrawal as he rowed the dinghy back to the yacht. When she had stepped up

on to the deck, he handed her the bucket of clams, then
the shovel.

'You're not coming abroad?'

'In a bit.' He moved the oars, sweeping away from
her. 'I'm going to explore the shore a bit first. Don't
wait up for me if I'm late back.'

He didn't look back until Dana had gone below
decks. He rowed steadily towards shore.

The beach was quiet, ringing with silence and
emptiness. He walked up the gentle slope, to the voyage
traced in the sand.

A fantasy voyage. She had asked him to take her on a
fantasy trip. And he had. He had described a trip to
her, taken her along the lines he drew on the sand.

She'd been with him, on board, every mile of the
way.

Next year, when he set sail from Vancouver, there
would be the ghost of a Danish girl on board. When he
put an ocean between them, would he have his ship to
himself?

CHAPTER NINE

IT was dark, the black dark of a moonless night, before Dana heard Kurt returning. She listened, lying quietly in her bunk.

The yacht shifted imperceptibly as he stepped on board, then she heard the click of the lifeline being fastened behind him. He was moving very quietly.

He didn't want to awaken her. He wanted her asleep, in her own bed.

Yesterday, on deck in Kurt's arms, she had lost all caution. She had cried out his name, declaring her love for him.

That was the last thing he wanted from her. No declarations of love—he'd made that clear. An affair, that was all. Just loving friends, but not love.

So it was over. Tomorrow, if he worked at it, he could get her home. Bull Harbour to Sointula wasn't impossible as a one-day sail—if he started early. One more day, then she'd be gone and Kurt would be free to continue his lonely life.

She slept badly, half waking several times in the night, finally opening her eyes with tears on her face, a desolate loneliness growing in her heart as the sound of the engine penetrated her consciousness. She lay with her eyes closed, listening to the moment the anchor touched the deck, to the shift of the engine sound as they got under way.

Part of her wanted to stay in her cabin, hiding from the day until she could step off this vessel. It was going to hurt, watching Kurt avoid her eyes through the hours ahead.

She got up, making her bunk, then starting breakfast in the galley before they came fully into the wind of the open channel.

Since leaving Queen Charlotte, they often ate together in the cockpit when they were under way. Today, Kurt ate in the cockpit while Dana ate her breakfast alone at the dinette table. Later, she went up to relieve Kurt at the wheel while he washed up the dishes.

The wind had been building steadily ever since they came into Galetas channel, the long corridor that led down to Port Hardy.

'Leave it on autopilot,' Kurt instructed her before he went down. 'If it starts to swing too much, call me and we'll reef the mains'l.'

Remembering her fight with the steering in the Hecate Strait, she followed his advice, letting the autopilot handle the tricky job of steering in a big following sea.

The waves were long and huge. They surged along with each wave. The wind, coming from behind, felt deceptively light because they were travelling with it. The sky had cleared to blue, but the wind was building enough that a small craft warning had been issued.

It wasn't a gale, certainly not enough to bother this ship, but it was a good wind for sailing. Freed from the cockpit by the autopilot, Dana went up on deck, standing in the wind with her hands in her pockets and her hair whipping wild about her face, letting the elements soothe the tension in her.

They were coming to the area where she could start to pick out landmarks. She hadn't been down Galetas channel often, but she recognised the lie of the land. She could pick out the islands, not recognising them, but pinpointing them from the chart and remembering how they looked from the other side—from the lighthouse at Pulteney Point.

She slipped down below once, briefly, to pour herself a cup of coffee. Kurt was at the dinette table, a pad of paper in front of him, a series of drawings spread around.

'Everything okay up there?' He didn't look up from the drawing.

'Fine. We're just passing Port Alexander.' It wasn't a port, really, but a long bay that made good anchorage. 'You don't want to stop there?'

'Too early to stop,' he told her, although they'd stopped early often enough when the impulse struck them to explore a particular bay. 'We'll go on.'

Dana hesitated before putting the lid back on the thermos. 'Do you want a cup of coffee?'

'No. You'd better get back up there—there'll be other boats in the channel.'

She was still at the wheel when they reached the bottom of Galetas. The wind shifted here, coming more on their port. To their right, Port Hardy beckoned. Dana altered course slightly to port, tightening the sails.

Kurt came up, feeling the change in their motion.

He stood beside her in the cockpit, looking around. 'Port Hardy?' he asked, nodding to their right.

'Yes. How's our course?' She meant, do you want to change course? They were headed on a course that would take them to the lighthouse in a few hours. She gestured to the other side of the wide strait they had entered. 'There's a multitude of inlets over there—you could explore it for months. Sure you don't want to sail over and look?'

'I'm sure.' He stepped towards the wheel, checking the set of the sails again with a glance. 'I'll take the watch now. I've made lunch for you—down below.'

'Are you in a hurry to take over? Before I change our course and take us somewhere else?'

'That's a danger, isn't it?' She had been smiling, but he wasn't. Her own smile died and she turned away, going down below to eat alone.

She couldn't stay below. She was restless, knew that soon she would do something silly—like pick a fight with Kurt, just to get some reaction from him, make him look her in the eyes. Or perhaps she would grab hold of him and beg him to love her, or to take her with him even if he couldn't love her.

She didn't think any of that showed when she returned to the cockpit. She smiled at him, a bright false smile, and told him, 'Keep the ship sailing level, will you?' I'm going out on the bowsprit.'

'Be careful.' His words of caution were almost automatic. He couldn't be worried; she'd been out there often enough in the weeks that had just passed.

'Of course.'

She wasn't about to take chances, but climbing out to the end of the bowsprit looked far more dangerous that it was. Dana held on carefully, leaning against the steel bars of the pulpit as she swung out around the stay that the jib flew from. When she was settled in her perch at the very end she linked her arms securely over the rails, because today was the wildest ride she had ever experienced out here on the bowsprit.

She was safe here, well wedged in, but exposed to every movement the yacht made. The water was right below her, pushing past, surging up towards her as the ship's bow dipped between waves.

Kurt shouted something at her and she waved, shaking her head because she could not hope to hear anything else but the water. If she shouted, he probably wouldn't hear her either. She was visible, but totally alone.

She leaned back and watched the sky waving closer, further, closer, felt the surge of gravity as the bows swept up on a wave and her body pressed hard against the pulpit.

They were sailing on the edge of the world. She closed her eyes to the motion, feeling, not seeing. A couple of hours' sailing and they could be in a secluded inlet on the far side of the strait. They could sail those inlets for weeks. It would make another article, another cruising ground for the series. She could suggest that to Kurt. She'd convinced him of other things in the past; surely if she talked, said the right words, he'd change his plans a little—just stretch this cruise by another few days.

She opened her eyes, almost believing she would find they had changed course. She was ready to see the far shore coming closer, the lighthouse moving farther away.

When she turned, she found herself staring at Pulteney Point.

Kurt was alone in the cockpit, with only his memories for company. He'd wanted her to leave him alone last night. It was painful, but she had to face the fact that last night—even after the passion they had shared—Kurt had preferred to be alone with his thoughts—his memories? Was it still Celeste? When he'd held Dana in his arms, had he wished——

Today was almost the end. If she turned her head, she could see the flash of the lighthouse. Still miles away, but coming closer. She closed her eyes and let herself float on the motion, gathering strength because the next few hours could be even harder.

When the wind picked up, her perch was no longer so comfortable. She climbed carefully back to the deck.

'You'll be home soon,' Kurt greeted her as she climbed into the cockpit.

She said nothing, staring out over the water.

'Why don't you give the lighthouse a call on the radio?'

She went back to the marine radio in the navigation room.

'Pulteney Point, *Windflower II*,' she called several times before her mother's familiar voice came back to her on the radio.

They changed to a working channel.

'Dana! Darling, we didn't expect you for at least another week! How lovely. Are you close? Can we see you yet?'

'We're just to the north, about eight miles—I'm sure you can see our sails if you look out of the living room window.'

'How long will you be? You'll be in today?'

'Two hours,' Kurt told her through the cockpit door.

'We'll be watching for you, dear,' her mother responded when the estimate was relayed to her. 'I'll have dinner ready for you both.'

Kurt was at the door again. 'There's no need for your mother to lay on dinner for me.'

Dana keyed the microphone. 'Fine, Mom. We'll be looking forward to it.'

'You have to come to dinner,' she told Kurt when her

mother had signed off. She didn't meet his eyes, but concentrated on getting the mike back on its hanger. 'My mother would be very disappointed if you didn't come. She loves cooking for people, loves having company.'

He said nothing, so she moved towards the doors. 'I guess I should go down to get my things together.'

He didn't stop her. Would the next few hours be like this? Dana watching each moment, every word, hoping Kurt would raise his hand, raise his eyes—change his mind. No, Dana. Don't leave. In her mind, those words had been on his lips fifty times today.

Packing took a while. She'd only brought a small pack on board, but her things were here and there throughout the boat. She collected her toothbrush from the head, a couple of pocket books from the bookcase. She hesitated over one. It was a spy story she had particularly enjoyed. She'd discussed the plot with Kurt and he had wanted to read it as well. He hadn't read it yet; somehow, they'd been too busy.

She opened the cover of the book. She found a pen and wrote on the inside cover, then replaced the book in his bookcase.

He hadn't wanted her to love him, but she couldn't stop. She had told him in a moment of passion that she loved him. Now she'd written it down. The words were there for him to read; he could throw the book out if he wanted.

She found she couldn't go back up on deck yet. She took down the brass lantern in the galley and painstakingly polished it to a warm shine. Kurt had left the galley immaculate when he cleaned up from their lunch. There was really nothing else that needed doing.

She moved from cabin to cabin, touching familiar

things—the carved box that contained Kurt's chess-men, the lanterns. She was saying goodbye, crying and telling herself she had to stop the tears.

How could she say goodbye to Kurt? He wouldn't touch her, wouldn't let her near. Today, they weren't even friends any more.

When she came back on deck, the lighthouse was large in front of them.

'We'll anchor just in front of the lighthouse,' Kurt was telling her, crisp and businesslike. 'That's where I dropped the hook the last time.'

It was an efficient operation. The anchor set easily in the sandy bottom, then he had the boat over the side and was directing Dana into it, getting her to shore quickly and efficiently.

'My, but you're brown, Dana!' Her mother had arms around her the moment her feet touched the sandy beach. Her father gave her a hug, then he was shaking Kurt's hand, limping a little as he walked up the beach with the dinghy painter to tie it to a nearby log.

'Tide's going out,' he told Kurt. 'No need to pull it any further up the beach. So, how did the testing go? Dana said in her letters that it went well, but tell me about that business with the windvane interface.'

'There they go,' said her mother, leading Dana towards the house. 'Just like men, off talking technical mumbo-jumbo the moment they see each other! Come on, dear. We'll get them coffee and see to supper. Tell me——'

Dana told her mother about Wendy and Wayne and Andy—Wendy's warm friendliness, her aversion to work. Wayne with his passion for computer talk. Andy with his friendly jokes, his almost embarrassing admiration for her.

'You look tired,' her mother said abruptly, in the midst of a description of the ride to the top of the mountain at Prince Rupert. 'You're tanned, but you don't really look well. Are you——'

'I'm fine. We just crossed from the Queen Charlottes—it took two days and my sleep got all turned around, standing watches as we crossed.'

Her mother frowned. 'You should go to bed now, Dana. Lie down for half an hour, get some rest before dinner.'

'I'm fine, really.' Kurt was still here, somewhere nearby with her father. When he was gone—that would be soon enough to hide in her room with the excuse of tiredness. 'Do you want these potatoes peeled, Mother?'

'Yes, those and—no, not like that, dear. Here, like this.'

When they were deeply involved in the details of dinner, her mother forgot that she had asked about Dana's look of exhaustion.

'Bruce must have taken him down to look at that generator,' Sherrie told her daughter when the men did not appear at once. 'Number two generator has been giving problems—your dad's been fighting with it all week.'

Dana looked out of the kitchen window, saw Kurt and her father outside the engine room, saw them begin to walk towards the house.

They were deep in conversation when they came through the kitchen door. Her father was unusually animated. Bruce and Kurt were both men who tended to listen more than they talked, but today they were talking eagerly with each other.

Their conversation was technical—about the trou-

blesome generator, about Kurt's autopilot system.
Dana followed most of it. If she'd tried, she could have
drawn herself into the talk.

She didn't try. The warmth in Kurt's eyes, his voice,
would cool if she came forward. He would withdraw.
She stayed in the kitchen, coming out to serve the men
coffee in the living room, acknowledging Kurt's thanks
with a smile.

She could hear from the kitchen. Listening, she could
claim Kurt's voice. She let herself imagine that they
were married, here on a visit to her parents.

The voice of the man I love, she told the stubborn eye
of one potato.

'They get on well, don't they?' her mother murmured
at her side.

'Yes.' Her father was always friendly, but this instant
affinity was unusual.

'I do like him,' her mother went on. 'Are you
sure——?'

'Mother, don't!' Dana forced her voice to stay low,
not to be overheard, but she spoke sharply to dampen
the speculation in her mother's eyes.

Her mother was past master at speaking low-voiced.
'Surely, Dana, when you've been alone together for the
last three weeks—sailing in that beautiful boat,
romantic inlets, and a really attractive man—
surely——'

'No!' she muttered. 'Mother, we can talk about the
weather, or even the trip I've just been on—but I don't
want to talk about the man! Please!'

Somehow that got through. Her mother shrugged.
'Just put that casserole back in the oven, would you,
Dana? Then you can take a cup of coffee yourself and
relax with the men.'

She went to change first. Kurt would be going soon. She wanted him to remember her looking nice.

She put on a long skirt with a clinging black top that contrasted effectively with her fair hair. Looking at herself in the full-length mirror in her room, she contemplated putting her hair up.

No. He liked her hair down, always enjoyed touching it, running his fingers through it.

'You look nice, dear,' her father told her as she re-entered the living room. 'I've always liked that outfit.'

Kurt said nothing, but Dana saw his eyes flicker before he glanced down at the book Bruce Hendricks was showing him.

Dana curled in the big easy chair across from Kurt. She was a whole room away from him, but she chose that chair because he couldn't look up without seeing her.

At dinner, her mother directed Kurt to the seat across from Dana. If he'd been sitting next to her, he couldn't have helped smelling the enticing perfume she had dabbed on to her pulse points. She brushed past him to get to her seat, her hair touching his cheek.

'Enough shop talk,' her mother announced as they began to eat. 'I want to know about the trip.' She had already heard some of it from Dana, but she wanted to know everything. She questioned Dana and Kurt. It wasn't really noticeable that although they both co-operated in telling the tale, they never really talked to each other.

'And Harold?' her mother demanded when they came to Queen Charlotte City. 'You did look up Harold, didn't you, Dana?'

'I saw him.'

'Where? Did you go out?'

Her mother would insist on all the details sooner of later. 'I ran into him in the hotel. Harold took me up the coast. He's got a house on the beach—quite impressive.'

Dana's eyes met Kurt's, her words almost freezing from the jealousy in his ice blue eyes.

She turned to her father, quickly changing the subject before her mother could get too carried away in her curiosity about Dana's love life.

'By the way, Dad, you'd have been fascinated by the Charlottes. The beaches up the coast are fantastic, miles and miles of hard-packed sand. Sometimes glass balls drift in. Beachcombing, searching for glass balls and agates, is a must for every tourist.'

'The Japanese fishermen use those glass balls.' Her father knew a good deal about them. Talking about them, he took everyone's attention off Dana.

She thought she might be deathly pale. Certainly her heart was pounding.

She'd only seen Kurt really angry that one night, when she came back from Harold. Then, in the darkened cockpit of his yacht, she hadn't seen his eyes but she had felt the full force of his fury with her. It had upset her for days afterwards.

Kurt hadn't forgotten. This time she could see his eyes, read how her disappearing with Harold had upset him. She hadn't expected that, could hardly believe the intensity of what she had seen.

Nothing happened, she wanted to tell him, but what could she say with her mother and father looking on?

A moment later his eyes were cool again. She almost believed she had imagined it.

Her mother started updating Dana on the activities of the local people. Dana was momentarily diverted by the latest news about Jon.

'I thought he was up north fishing?'

'He's back now. Cohoe salmon season is closed, and they're all getting into this hang-gliding thing now they've got some spare time.'

She couldn't help being interested in the idea of taking to the air currents like a bird.

'Where are they doing it? They need a good hill, a cliff.'

'Up on the hill behind the old Jensen homestead.'

It was something to think about. Perhaps she would stay on here for a time. Her parents would certainly welcome her staying, and she might regain some enthusiasm for the book she'd been planning. Riding the air currents could ease the loneliness that would surely come now. How could she be heartbroken floating high above the world?

When dinner was over, Kurt let her mother press another cup of coffee on him. He would be up late tonight, Dana speculated, because he usually avoided more than a couple of cups of coffee in the evening hours.

The inevitable moment came when he covered his cup with his hand, refusing another refill.

'I'd better get back.' He was already getting to his feet.

'There's no need,' her mother protested. 'Why not stay the night here? We have an extra room, and we'd love to have you.'

'Thank you, but I must get on.'

'Tonight?' Dana protested in a high voice. 'You're sailing tonight?'

'Yes.'

'But it's dark!'

'There's the radar,' he reminded her, 'and it's time I was on my way.'

Time he left Dana. She knew that was what he meant.

'How far will you go? Into Sointula?' He could safely anchor off the lighthouse all night, but he surely knew that. He wanted to get away from her, get her out of sight before he slept.

'Down the channel a way.' He shrugged.

'I'll walk you to the beach,' she told him. She couldn't stop him, but she couldn't bring herself to say the word goodbye yet. Just a few moments more. She caught her mother's eye and knew that she had given herself away. When she came back, there would be her mother's matchmaking curiosity to deal with.

Her father was shaking hands with Kurt, issuing an open invitation for him to return any time. Dana and Kurt would be alone on their last brief walk.

There was so much to say, yet she walked silently at his side. She was so close to him, but not touching. He could easily have caught her hand in his, but he didn't. When they reached his dinghy she said his name, hardly loud enough to be heard.

He stopped, turning to her, smoothing her hair with his hands, holding her head lightly.

'This hang-gliding thing—are you going to get involved in it, Dana?'

'I don't know.' What did it matter when Kurt was leaving her? 'I suppose I will. I won't be sailing, so——'

'You'll be careful, won't you? Those things can be dangerous. I wouldn't want you hurt.'

She closed her eyes. This wasn't fair, not fair at all. 'Kurt, if you want some say in what I do, then don't leave.'

She couldn't breathe. She was waiting, willing him to take her with him . . . and knowing he was about to say a final farewell.

He stared at her in the moonlight a long moment before he said anything at all.

'You know, Dana,' he told her softly, 'you don't need the feminine accessories—the alluring scent, the sexy clothes—you're already irresistible without any of that.'

'Will I see you again?' she whispered as a fishing boat steamed past the point with his searchlight sweeping the water.

'No.'

She touched his face, feeling the faint roughness because it would be the last time. 'Then I'm not irresistible, am I? If I were, you wouldn't be leaving me behind.' She took a quick, shaky breath. 'Do you have to leave me, Kurt?'

He was bending to kiss her, but his lips were so still on hers that she knew before he said, 'Yes, Danish girl.'

'Kurt, about Harold——'

'Don't, Dana. It doesn't matter.'

'It does matter. I saw your eyes tonight when Mother asked me about him. You were——'

'Jealous as hell,' he told her with a short, bitter laugh. 'Waiting for you that night, knowing—yes, I was jealous. But you were right, absolutely right. I had no right. It was totally irrational.'

Not if he loved her. It would be perfectly understandable if he loved her.

'Kurt, if Harold has anything to do with your feeling you have to leave—if that's any part of it, then you should know what happened that night——'

His fingers bit into her scalp as he kissed her hard

and quickly, then he stepped back, leaving her alone and shivering on the beach.

His voice was low and bitter. 'If it hurt, there was no one to blame but myself. When you walked out of that dining-room with him, would you have gone if I had asked you to stay?'

'No.' Harold had only been a futile attempt to soothe her own painful love for Kurt.

'I knew that—while I was imagining you and him, I knew I could have stopped you. No, Dana, Harold has nothing to do with my leaving. If anything it makes leaving harder—picturing you in someone else's arms.'

'Then, Kurt——'

'I can't do it again, Danish girl. If I let you, you'd be more necessary to me than breathing.' His hand reached out, but he didn't touch her at all.

His voice was only a whisper, but his words echoed around her long after he had left her alone on the beach.

'If I let myself love you, Danish girl, how could I ever survive losing you?'

CHAPTER TEN

DANA watched Kurt's lights until they disappeared among the navigation markers to the south. She turned away when she could no longer pretend to see him.

Where would he stop tonight? He'd tire eventually and put in—where? Boat Bay—the little anchorage the fishermen liked to crowd into? He might go further, closer to Seymour Narrows.

She couldn't go back to the house, to her mother's questions. She went to the light-tower, climbing the circular stairs inside, emerging outside at the top, leaning against the rail and watching the lights to the south.

When she climbed back down she could feel a numbness growing inside her. Not pain, only an empty void.

Her father was in the kitchen, adjusting the flame on the oil stove for the night.

'Where's Mom?' she asked.

'She's gone to bed.'

The clock above the sink said it was almost midnight. How long ago had Kurt gone? How far away was he?

'Are you all right?' She could see the concern in her father's eyes.

'Don't I look all right?'

'No.'

Her emotions had always been there for him to read on her face.

169

'Kurt's gone?'

She nodded. She poured herself a cup of coffee. It would keep her awake, but that hardly mattered. 'You liked him, didn't you, Dad?'

'Very much.'

The coffee was black and strong. She stared at it. 'So did I.'

He took the cup away from her. 'You don't need that. Get some sleep.'

Amazingly, there were no dreams this time, just the heavy sleep of exhaustion.

Dana was awake early, up and dressed and seeking coffee in the kitchen—the galley, she'd almost called it in her mind.

'Morning, darling,' her mother greeted her. 'Did you sleep well?'

'Fair,' she replied, because there was no point pretending when her mother's eyes showed that faint worry.

'He'll be back,' her mother told her. Sherrie Hendricks didn't miss much, but she was a dreamer.

'No, he won't. You're right if you're thinking I've fallen in love with him, but he left because he wanted to leave. He doesn't plan to come back.'

'Last night he couldn't keep his eyes off you.'

If that was true it was news to Dana. She had ben watching him and he had hardly met her eyes all evening.

'I don't want to talk about it—please. And don't cook breakfast for me. I'm not hungry. I think I'll go and work in the garden for a while.'

She made it into a busy day, weeding the garden, digging some clams on the beach, helping her father overhaul the troublesome generator in the engine room.

For most of the time, she stayed out of the kitchen,
stayed away from private conversations with her
mother. Today she was doing tasks for the hands,
keeping her brain and her heart on hold.

Warren would be expecting her application for that
job in the news department. She hadn't sent it, hadn't
even started to work on her résumé.

Kurt had said the job wasn't for her.

Kurt said she must be careful if she went hang-
gliding.

It wasn't Celeste any more; she was almost sure of
that. Once, in Bishop Bay, he had turned away from her
because she was not Celeste. Not any more. Last night,
when he walked away from her, it had nothing to do
with Celeste, except that she was the one who had
taught him the pain of loss—Celeste and their daughter
Patricia.

She knew there was no way she could fully
understand what he had felt on losing his family, but
she could not believe it was better to live alone than to
take the risk of loving.

Dana and her father were both covered with grease
and oil by the time the generator was back in one piece.

'I think we've got it,' he told her with some
satisfaction as they started putting away tools.

'Good.' She handed him a large spanner and
watched as he placed it in its place.

They walked out of the engine room. Out on the grass
the noise of the engines seemed far away. The sky was
full of stars—a sailor's night.

'Your mother and I,' he began hesitantly, 'have been
wondering about your plans.'

'I've been wondering about my plans, too.' All day
working, trying not to think, feeling an imperative

question weighing on her.

'We're hoping that you'll stay at home—for a while, I mean. I know you've your own life to lead, but there's no rush, is there?'

Dana needed people who loved her nearby. He knew she was hurt. Unlike her mother, he wouldn't say much, but he wanted her close by to care for.

'Kurt was married before.' Her voice was clear on the night air. 'His wife and daughter—they died three years ago in a fire.'

The beam of the light swept in a circle over the glassy water, cut a white band of light through the trees on the island.

'He doesn't want to love anyone. He thinks it's better not to take the risk. Do you think he's right?'

He took her arm and she felt his limp as they started to walk. 'Even if I lost your mother tomorrow, I wouldn't have missed the years with her for anything.' He squeezed her arm gently. 'Now tell me what you've decided.'

'I should sit here, shouldn't I? Waiting, hoping he'll come back. Mother thinks he'll be back.'

'And you?' He started her walking slowly towards the house.

'Maybe it's possible, but I can't take the chance. If I sit here, waiting, I could grow old with loneliness.'

A sea-bird called across the glassy water. Soon it would be dark. 'I think he'd be through Seymour Narrows on this tide. I thought of getting Eddie Wainwright with his seaplane—begging a ride from him, searching down the passage—all the little bays. Well, I know it's crazy. I know how hard it is to spot one particular boat from the air—but that's the sort of thing that's been going through my mind today. I feel a terrible need to do something active.'

She could see her mother in the kitchen window. Her mother loved the kitchen, loved working at the window where she could watch the maritime world sail past the lighthouse point.

'I guess, though, that if I found him in some bay down the coast I might not be welcome—I certainly wasn't invited. So I'd better play it cooler. I've got the articles to finish, then commentaries to write. Once that's done, I should go down to Vancouver to record the commentaries in the studio.'

'Kurt's going to Vancouver?'

'Yes. It should take him about four or five days, don't you think? I do know where he's berthing when he gets there. I'll stop by to see him.'

She could tell from her father's eyes that her plans troubled him, but he made no attempt to talk her out of following Kurt to Vancouver.

And then what? If he was going to Montreal, perhaps she should think about that. What was the job situation in French Canada?

He had said she was irresistible. It wasn't true, because he had left, but it must mean she had a pretty good chance—if she kept trying, didn't give up.

She worked on the article the next morning, then finished it in the afternoon. It was slower going using the old portable typewriter instead of Kurt's computer.

She took the speedboat and ran over to mail the article in Sointula. Then she started on the commentaries.

She gave herself two days of hard work to complete the commentaries. Then she went back into Sointula, picked up her car, and caught the ferry over to Vancouver Island.

Driving seemed strange after so many weeks cruising, but she found herself driving into the queue for the Nanaimo to Vancouver ferry in record time. She had been thinking ahead as she drove, calculating when Kurt might arrive at the marina—today or tomorrow, she thought.

She spent the ferry trip to Vancouver on the upper deck, thinking how tame it was steaming across Georgia Strait in this big vessel, hardly feeling the waves.

'Kurt Saunders, you are not going to get rid of me this easily,' she told the seagulls. She remembered his arms around her, his passionate need of her, his face across the chess board—so many memories.

But she was unprepared for the bitterness of her disappointment when she arrived at the Andersons' marina to find *Windflower II* had not yet arrived.

She fought her way back through the rush hour traffic, registered in a small motel and phoned Warren.

Warren liked getting things done early. They made arrangements for Dana's recording session first thing the next morning.

It was almost like being in a strange city, pacing the motel room restlessly in the evening, going out for dinner and another check of the marina—no sign of Kurt.

Dana checked the marina again the next morning before driving into the city centre for her recording session.

Could Kurt possibly have changed his plans? He could easily have put into another city—Victoria, perhaps, where good sailing winds blew perpetually in Juan de Fuca Strait.

She came back to herself with a snap when she heard

the blaring horns, saw the white car miss her front bumper by inches. She'd gone into a crazy trance, driven right through a red light, started every hothead within a block blazing away at his horn.

She had to concentrate, keep her mind on the driving, not on the tall blond man who'd become such a crucial part of her life. Her hands were shaking, her heart pounding, but she got the car going again, drove away from the intersection slowly and steadily, watching carefully for everything—lights, cars, pedestrians.

She certainly wasn't surprised when she heard the siren, saw the flashing red and blue lights in her rear view mirror. She pulled over, holding her breath, hoping the police car would pass by, pursuing some other law-breaker.

He didn't. The car pulled up behind her, the lights still flashing as the officer got out.

She'd heard it was good psychology to get out of the car, walk back to the police car and meet the uniformed man on a more equal footing. But she couldn't have stood if her life depended on it. Her legs would be rubber. She wound her window down.

'May I see your licence and registration, miss?' He was probably no older than her, wearing a solemnity that took the place of age.

Her glove compartment was full of papers—some letters from home, the stub of an old pay cheque.

'I know it's here,' she assured him, rummaging for the paper proof of her ownership and insurance. Finally she found it and handed the form up with her driver's licence for the policeman's silent inspection.

He handed the papers back.

'Do you realise that you were doing sixty-three in a

fifty-kilometre zone? You went through a red light—
you're extrememly lucky there wasn't an accident!'

She deserved every bit of the lecture he gave her. No
one should be driving with her mind as far away as
Dana's had been.

She signed for the ticket that he finally gave her,
promised to drive more carefully, and drove on very
cautiously.

She had to stop for a cup of coffee before she went
into the studio to meet Warren, but somehow she got
through the recording session with Warren smiling his
approval of her work.

'I haven't seen your application yet, Dana. Dead-
line's tomorrow, you know.'

'Thanks, Warren, but I don't think it's my thing.' As
always, she found the station atmosphere a stimulating
change from the rest of the world, but Kurt had been
right. As a daily diet, she couldn't take this tension and
constant high drama. 'I'm going to do some serious
writing. I think I'll be leaving the city.'

'You're not stopping the commentaries?'

'No, but I don't need to live here for that, do I? I can
come in just to record, or even record over the
telephone from home. I'm planning to start working on
a book. I want to keep up my freelance contacts, too,
but I'll just be visiting, not living here.'

The revenue from her articles and the commentaries
would keep her for some months if she was careful. She
hoped to be somewhere near Kurt, but even if she
couldn't follow Kurt she would not return to the city.

She had checked out of the motel room that morning,
had no real plans except to wait for Kurt. Though it was
really too early in the day to expect his arrival, she
drove back to the marina. She would just check quickly

before finding a restaurant for lunch.

She recognised the wooden masts from the car park—beautiful varnished masts, far more beautiful to her than the white-painted aluminium of most of the other sailboats nearby.

Some of the more modern marinas had installed locked gates with slots for plastic cards to unlock the gate. Not this one. It was older, quaint, a little run down, but comfortable. No one stopped Dana as she walked on to the floats.

There were a few people around working on their boats, some lazily soaking up the sun on deck. One bearded sailor sat back from his painting to watch her intently for a moment.

The yacht was deserted, the doors locked. She would probably remember the combination to his boat for the rest of her life. She dialed the numbers and opened the doors, placing the lock on its hook in the passageway.

There was a pot of coffee on the diesel stove, an unwashed plate at the sink. Dana hung her jacket in the locker. She could feel Kurt. He would be back any minute.

She moved around the boat. Kurt hadn't made up his bed this morning—the bedclothes were evidence of a restless night. The computer was still installed in the cabin that had been hers. She'd been afraid he would have moved it to erase that small sign of her presence.

Ever since she left Sointula the day before she had been trying to rehearse the words she would use.

I love you, Kurt. I can't face a whole life without you. You feel something for me—I know you do. I'm not asking for a commitment. I know you don't want that, but just let me stay. As long as you still feel something for me, let me stay.

Feeling was what Kurt didn't want. He wanted safety, not love.

She had to do something while she waited. She hadn't even the status of guest, but she filled the sink with water and did his few breakfast dishes before she went out to sit in the cockpit, to watch for him.

She heard cars come and go in the car park. When the taxi drove up, she knew that it would be Kurt. She caught a brief glimpse of his fair hair as he came down the ramp, then he disappeared. She could hear his footsteps, knew when he stopped to talk to someone although she could not see him.

Then he was closer, walking towards her. He would see her any minute now. Her throat was freezing, drying up. She couldn't say a word.

She met his eyes when he stepped on to the deck. He was dressed for the city, warm brown slacks topped with a soft cashmere sweater, a fashionable sports jacket protecting him from the autumn chill.

His eyes were black with some emotion that might well be anger. He crossed the deck, stepped down into the cockpit.

Dana was sitting, couldn't even get to her feet.

'I thought you must have gone out for groceries,' she said at last. His arms were empty.

'I was at the airport.'

'Getting tickets? You're leaving for Montreal already?' There wasn't anything she could think of to say, to convince him she should come with him.

'I was trying for a standby seat on a plane. The plane was full.' He was frowning. She had been insane to think he would want her here. He'd told her clearly enough that it was over. Nothing had changed.

'It's cool out here,' she told him at last, nervously. She

stood up. 'Could we go inside?' Her jacket was inside, and her bag.

Kurt followed her silently. That first day, when he had shown her the yacht, she had followed him, knowing he was a man she could follow to the ends of the world.

He wouldn't let her. In Montreal, how could she get near him if he did not want her?

'I've been thinking,' she told him, her voice strengthening as she got the words started—if she didn't look at him, she could talk well enough. 'You're leaving. You'll be away from here for a few months. You'll need someone to look after this boat, and I need a place to live—I could stay here, on board. I could rent her from you, just until you come back.'

When he came back, she'd be waiting. Perhaps he would let her come with him when he went cruising again.

The silence in the salon was deafening. When Kurt spoke, she turned back to face him. His voice was low, strangely gravelly.

'When I left you at the lighthouse, I knew you'd still be haunting me.'

'Haunting?' She wanted to be sharing life with him, not haunting him as a dead woman might.

'I've been wanting you so much, for so long. I knew the wanting wouldn't stop the moment I sailed away. I dropped the hook in a little place called Boat Bay the first night. I sat on deck for a long time in the dark, looking back up the channel as if I'd be able to see your lighthouse. I came damned close to pulling the hook up and sailing back to you.'

'I told myself it would take a while before I stopped missing you, but I'd get my balance back—it was as if

I'd lost possession of myself, but I'd get it back if I just kept going.

'I went through Seymour Narrows at full flood tide. I must have been mad! Thirteen knots current at the peak on that tide. It was a hell of a ride.'

'Why?' Kurt was the man who didn't take chances, didn't take risks unless they were well calculated.

'I had to make myself feel something, anything that you weren't part of.'

She should never have come. She had no right to pursue him when he wanted so badly to be free of her.

'Did it work?' she asked.

He laughed harshly. 'I was feeling, all right! When I hit the edge of that whirlpool where Ripple Rock used to be before they blasted it out, I thought I'd get caught and lose control of the vessel entirely. I probably wasn't in that much danger, but there was a moment when I thought I might not get through. When I did come shooting out the other end of the narrows, there was only one thing on my mind. If I'd killed myself with that stupid stunt, I'd never have seen you again.'

'You told me you didn't *want* to see me again.'

'That's what I told myself for the rest of the trip down here. I couldn't wait to get here, to get off this boat and away, somewhere we'd never shared. You've no idea how deeply you've worked your way into my life on this yacht. Whenever I took down a sail, I had to stop myself calling you to come and help. When I passed your cabin, I would look in, just to say hello and reassure myself that you were nearby. Last night, I actually got out the chess board and set it up.

'You spent only one night in my bed, but I couldn't sleep there without dreaming you were at my side. By the time I pulled into this marina this morning, I thought I might have to sell this boat to stop seeing you every time I went sailing.'

She had wanted to get under his skin until he couldn't ignore her as an important part of his life. She hadn't wanted this, though—hadn't wanted to be the image he ran from.

'I shouldn't have come,' she sighed. 'I didn't want to haunt you. I don't want to be another ghost for you to carry around.'

'It wouldn't have made any difference. I've been fooling myself, Dana. I went into the city. I've always enjoyed this city—maybe because the ocean's right there, on the doorstep. Today was different. There were two million people around me, but the streets were empty.'

Dana turned away. 'So you had to get further away? You had to get back to Montreal so fast that you couldn't even stop to empty your coffee pot or do your dishes?' That wasn't at all like Kurt, He liked a clean ship.

'I didn't get on the morning flight—I was next in line for a cancellation, but no one cancelled. I did manage to get a ticket on this afternoon's flight.'

He would be gone in a few hours.

She moved away from him, to the hanging locker. Her hand closed on her jacket.

She was concentrating on getting out before the tears started. The last thing she expected was for him to move a hand to touch her. She swung around, facing him with anger growing protectively over her hurt.

'If you want me to go, then don't touch me. I'll be out of here——'

'I'm not asking you to go.' He was pushing something into her hand. 'I don't need this now.'

She opened the airline folder, stared at the almost incomprehensible letters and numbers written on the ticket inside.

'Port Hardy?' she queried.

'They don't fly jets into Sointula. That was as close as I could get. I phoned a seaplane company in Port Hardy and arranged for a charter to take me over to the lighthouse before dark tonight.'

Dana was staring at the ticket, not sure what he was telling her, afraid to believe it was what she wanted to hear.

'You could have sailed back.'

He shook his head. His fingers were touching her hair, gently drawing it back from her face. Who had said that hair had no feeling? 'Sailing is not the way to travel when you have to get somewhere fast.'

'But why?'

Kurt was drawing her closer. His hands, tangled in her hair, were bringing her face closer. His lips touched hers. His fingers found her scalp, massaging with sensuous finger tips. Her words of protest meant nothing. It didn't matter if it was only for a moment or an hour. She would grasp every moment of closeness he would allow her.

His hands slid down, laying a claim on her body. She slid her arms around his neck, opening her lips to him, melting her body against his.

They caught fire from the touch of each other. The gentle kiss turned to a wild, demanding passion with a suddenness that sent Dana spinning, hardly knowing when Kurt drew her down on to the settee.

When his lips moved away from hers, his hands stilled on her, she found herself lying in his arms, staring at his face only inches away.

His eyes were a deep rich blue. The lines of his face were deep from nights of poor sleep. His mouth was open slightly, his shallow breathing revealing the effect of her nearness on him.

'You shouldn't do this,' she told him. 'You said you didn't want to lay a claim on me—but if you touch me again, I'll be yours for ever whether you want me or not.'

'Shush,' he told her softly. 'I know what I said—I talked a lot of nonesense. Danish girl, I'm trying to tell you that I love you.' He touched the side of her face, drawing his fingertips down her cheek to her sensitive throat.

'I know I'm not doing a very good job of it. I don't have a lot of practice. I can't remember anyone being around to love when I was a kid. Celeste was my one venture into love. When she died, I turned my back on that part of life. These last few months, I've been so busy being frightened of loving, of being vulnerable to you, that I didn't see what was happening to me.'

His hands were moving gently on her back, telling her the same message his eyes held.

'What was happening to you?' If she traced the lines of his forehead, they smoothed to her touch.

He touched her lips with the faintest trace of a kiss. 'You were around all the time, every day, and I didn't realise. The sun was getting brighter in the sky, turning the darkest shadows to light—even the shadows in my heart. At first, when I left you on that lighthouse, I thought it was a longing that would pass.

'The world was grey—all the colours toned down. I could enjoy sailing, but the spark was gone. Tearing down Seymour Narrows, I thought I could force some excitement back into life. It took a while, but this morning I finally realised what had been staring me in the face for a long time. All the depth and colour that made life worth living—all that came from you. I was afraid of loving you—but when I left you I left all the joy, all the light in life. I was crazy, thinking I wanted to live alone. I knew that this morning, looking at the grey world.

'I kept remembering the day I left you—I had other memories too, every moment we've ever spent together—but that day was what I was thinking of as I came back here just now. I was at your parents' house talking in the living-room with your father. I could see you in the kitchen with your mother, then sitting across from me. I kept slipping out of reality, looking across at you and seeing you as my wife, the two of us visiting your parents—not just you and I, but kids too. I could see our children—a boy and a girl. They were blond and beautiful—they'd have to be blond, wouldn't they, with us for parents? I could hear them playing down the hall as I talked to Bruce. You'll think I'm crazy, but whenever I looked up and saw you, I thought that later we'd say good night, go to our own room.'

'I don't think you're crazy.' If they were going to be together, it made no sense at all for her to be crying.

'I've no idea what you think about children. We haven't had time to talk about them, but——' He found the tears on her face, started to kiss them away.

'Can we take them sailing?' she asked him. 'You'll let me come on that cruise with you, won't you? I want your child, Kurt. When you made love to me, I don't think there's any chance I'd have got pregnant, but I've been wishing there was. If you were walking away from me, it would have helped a little to have your child.'

'I've hurt you,' he said as his lips touched the corner

of her mouth. 'Let me make that up to you. Let me love you, darling. Let me share your life with you.' He took her lips in a deep kiss.

She was settled in the curve of his arm, holding his head down, deepening their kiss. Her head fell back as his lips traced along her neck and found the fullness above her breasts.

'Tell me you love me,' he groaned as he opened her blouse and found the evidence of her arousal. 'I need you to tell me you love me, Danish girl!'

'I've always loved you,' she whispered to him. 'The first time I saw you, I thought I could follow you to the ends of the earth.'

'Just be with me, Dana. I love you—need you so badly, my darling. I'm not a young boy in my twenties any more—I never expected to feel like this—God, Dana! I've never felt so off balance, so badly in need of anything in my life. We'll go sailing, you wild creature, and you can write your novel while we cross the Pacific. But we'll have our home, too. Somewhere on the water, on the north end of the Island. We'll bring *Windflower II* back here when we've had enough wandering for a while, moor her in our own bay where we can see her from our window.'

'Yes,' she consented, returning his kiss, sliding her hands under his sweater so that she could touch the warmth of him.

'Kurt, about Harold——'

'No——'

'Hush, you jealous man!' She slipped her hands up along his chest, silenced him with her lips. 'I never thought you'd be so jealous. Nothing happened, Kurt. I took my stockings off to walk in the sand. And my make-up—he kissed me and I really tried to want him—I was hurting so badly from your not wanting me. But it wasn't his arms I wanted around me. I started crying in the end, and that cooled his ardour somewhat.'

'I don't deserve that,' he told her in a husky voice. 'I should never have let you walk away from me. If I'd had the guts to admit to myself that I loved you——'

'Then love me, Kurt,' she urged him. 'Love me now.'

He couldn't tell her properly with words. He showed her, with his hands and his lips, with every part of his body, that he would love her for all the days of their life.

NOV 1986 HARDBACK TITLES

ROMANCE

When Love Flies By *Jeanne Allan*	2628	0 263 11239 X
Bride on Approval *Elizabeth Ashton*	2629	0 263 11240 3
The Marriage Deal *Sara Craven*	2630	0 263 11241 1
The Wrong Mirror *Emma Darcy*	2631	0 263 11242 X
Out of the Blue *Mons Daveson*	2632	0 263 11243 8
Shadows *Vanessa Grant*	2633	0 263 11244 6
All My Tomorrows *Rosemary Hammond*	2634	0 263 11245 4
Loving *Penny Jordan*	2635	0 263 11246 2
Fascination *Patricia Lake*	2636	0 263 11247 0
Love in the Dark *Charlotte Lamb*	2637	0 263 11248 9
In Love with the Man *Marjorie Lewty*	2638	0 263 11249 7
Out of the Shadows *Sandra Marton*	2639	0 263 11250 0
Exclusive Contract *Dixie McKeone*	2640	0 263 11251 9
Beware of Married Men *Elizabeth Oldfield*	2641	0 263 11252 7
Beyond Her Control *Jessica Steele*	2642	0 263 11253 5
Moroccan Madness *Angela Wells*	2643	0 263 11254 3

MASQUERADE HISTORICAL ROMANCE

The Briar Rose *Dinah Dean*	M155	0 263 11315 9
The Wild Heart *Anne Herries*	M156	0 263 11316 7

TEMPTATION

Lifetime Affair *Patt Parrish*	0 263 11319 1
The Wings of Morning *Jackie Weger*	0 263 11320 5

DOCTOR NURSE ROMANCE

A Surgeon's Hands *Jennifer Eden*	D73	0 263 11317 5
Hong Kong Surgeon *Margaret Barker*	D74	0 263 11318 3

LARGE PRINT

No Other Love *Mary Lyons*	127	0 263 11267 5
Nurse Bryony *Rhona Trezise*	128	0 263 11268 3
Secret Fire *Violet Winspear*	129	0 263 11269 1

DEC 1986 HARDBACK TITLES

———— ROMANCE ————

The Waiting Heart *Jeanne Allan*	2644	0 263 11273 X
Golden Bay *Gloria Bevan*	2645	0 263 11274 8
Rose-Coloured Love *Amanda Carpenter*	2646	0 263 11275 6
Gathering of Eagles *Angela Carson*	2647	0 263 11276 4
Street Song *Ann Charlton*	2648	0 263 11277 2
Recipe for Love *Kay Clifford*	2649	0 263 11278 0
The Unpredictable Man *Emma Darcy*	2650	0 263 11279 9
Song in a Strange Land *Diana Hamilton*	2651	0 263 11280 2
The Married Lovers *Flora Kidd*	2652	0 263 11281 0
Prisoner of Shadow Mountain *Mariel Kirk*	2653	0 263 11282 9
Stairway to Destiny *Miriam Macgregor*	2654	0 263 11283 7
Sleeping Tiger *Joanna Mansell*	2655	0 263 11284 5
A Rogue and a Pirate *Carole Mortimer*	2656	0 263 11285 3
The Love Artist *Valerie Parv*	2657	0 263 11286 1
Sunset at Izilwane *Yvonne Whittal*	2658	0 263 11287 X
Bride of Diaz *Patricia Wilson*	2659	0 263 11288 8

 HISTORICAL ROMANCE

In Love and War *Mary Nichols*	M157	0 263 11339 6
Gypsy Royal *Hazel Smith*	M158	0 263 11340 X

TEMPTATION

True Colours *Jayne Ann Krentz*	0 263 11361 2
Star-Crossed *Regan Forest*	0 263 11362 0

DOCTOR NURSE ROMANCE

A Surgeon at St Mark's *Elizabeth Harrison*	D75	0 263 11337 X
No Ordinary Nurse *Sarah Franklin*	D76	0 263 11338 8

LARGE PRINT

Tropical Eden *Kerry Allyne*	130	0 263 11270 5
Year's Happy Ending *Betty Neels*	131	0 263 11271 3
The Scorpio Man *Claudia Jameson*	132	0 263 11272 1

Welcome
to the Wonderful World
of Mills & Boon Romance

For the incurable romantic — the best variety in tender love stories, from far away places to modern hospitals or even the romantic past.

Travel all over the world with contemporary heroes and heroines as their love affair carries them to a happy ending. Step back in time as centuries of intrigue, discovery and conquest become the backdrop to historical passion. Share the drama and excitement of the medical profession while doctors and nurses find time for love in busy hospitals and crowded surgeries.

Every month, Mills & Boon publishes a wide range of new hardback titles across all its series, with sixteen contemporary Romances, two Masquerade Historical Romances, two Doctor/ Nurse Romances, as well as three Large Print Romances.

The most appealing love stories from the best romantic authors and the most experienced publisher of romance — Mills & Boon is the Rose of Romance.

We sincerely hope you enjoyed reading this Mills & Boon Romance.

Yours truly,
THE PUBLISHERS
Mills & Boon Romances